Beautiful Heart

By

ALYSIA S. KNIGHT

Heart Dreams PRESS

Beautiful Heart

By Alysia S. Knight
Published by Heart Dreams Press
Copyright © 2017 Alysia S. Knight
Cover design: by Kelli Ann Morgan @
www.inspirecreativeservices.com

ISBN:1-942000-21-9
ISBN-13:978-1-942000-21-1

Also available from Alysia S. Knight

ଔ

Past To Die For

Temperature Rising

Kare for Me

Blind Witness

Beauty and the Chief

Trail to Her Heart

His Governess

Her Brand of Trouble

The Ruins – Out of Time

My Spy

Whistleblower

Mindblower

Where There's a Will

ଔ

For all those who have waited patiently for me to get back on my feet. Thank you for your love and support.

Alysia S. Knight

Chapter One

"Come're girl." The gruff voice of Silas Marsh grounded out.

Eliza side-stepped, putting the desk in between her and her stepfather.

The furrows in his brow deepened, but the gleam in his eyes picked up as they played down her body.

Shivers of revulsion made her tremble as she shook her head.

"Don't go disobeying me." The threat was as clear as his intent if she came within reach.

She edged back as he took a step forward. What was he doing there? He was supposed to be gone for the day. He'd left with her mother only twenty minutes earlier.

"Don't be thinkin' that whelp brother of yours is going to come in here. I locked the door."

"Where's my mother?"

"Your stepmother is visiting that old harpy cousin of mine. You don't be needin' to worry. I've plenty of time before I have to be fetchin' her."

Eliza eased farther away. "I'll get out of here then. I can do the polishing later." She made a dash to the door. She was a couple feet from it when powerful, stubby fingers locked on her arm, jerking her around to meet him face to face.

"You'll be stayin'."

She flinched as much from the sour smell of his breath as from the threatening words, but it was the words that drove terror into her heart.

"Eliza." The sound of her brother, Matthew's voice brought her a surge of hope.

"Don't be thinkin' it. He won't be interruptin' like in the past."

"Stay away from me!" Taking him by surprise, she jerked back and broke away, darting around the chair, which wasn't much of a barrier because, unfortunately, he was between her and the door.

The rumble that came from the man was supposed to be a laugh, but there was no humor in it for her. Eliza glanced at the door, calculating her chances of making it there and turning the lock before Silas could reach her.

"Don't be thinkin' me a monster. It's all your fault. You might look like an angel, but you're a temptress of the devil. You can't even walk down the street without makin' a man want you. Benedict Cooper and Ellis Woolworth have both been by in the past week askin' for your hand. You leading them on?"

Eliza shook her head. "I haven't done anything to encourage them."

"Don't be lyin' girl. I suppose you don't want to marry any of them askin' after you."

Eliza thought of the men she knew who had showed interest in her, Benedict, Ellis, John, and Simon. There were several others. None stood out in her mind over another, but any would be favorable to get her out of the house and away from her stepfather. In the two months Silas Marsh had been married to her stepmother, he'd become obsessive in his pursuit of her. It was only a matter of time until he managed to catch her unprotected.

"You can arrange a marriage if you want, then you wouldn't have to support me." Eliza knew her father had left plenty for her support and a decent dowry, though she doubted she'd ever see it.

"Now, why would I be wantin' to saddle a man with a temptress like you?" He stepped toward her.

Eliza didn't realize the wall was behind her until she bumped against it. She cried when he grabbed her again, pulling her toward him.

"You're of the devil. Make a man think impure thoughts just lookin' at you. Golden like an angel, but it's all a lie."

"No." She shook her head in denial.

"Eliza!"

She jumped as Matthew called her name again.

"You yell and I'll tan the whelp's hide. You're getting what you deserve." He gave a hard yank, pulling her off balance. She fell against his bulk.

"No!" She struck out. Flailing her arms, her hand cut across Marsh's nose. With a grunt, he stumbled back. Released, she turned to flee, but didn't make it as a blow struck her across the cheek sending her into the wall.

Dark eyes glinted out of a reddened face. "Harlot." He grabbed her by the back of her neck and spat the words in her face. "How dare you strike me? Evil just as I declared. You should have been taught to respect your elders. Time you need a lesson."

Eliza cringed as much from the words as his raised hand.

"Eliza, I found you." Matthew's head popped above the window sill. I told you I would."

"Get out of here, boy." Silas glared at the open window.

"I can't. Mama said Eliza was to help me do my ciphering before she gets back. Come on, Eliza, we got to get started now. If we don't, I won't finish, then I won't get my dessert and Mama made plum pudding." He crawled over the windowsill before Silas could say anything else.

Threat and promise slashed through his eyes as Silas peered back at her. "Don't be thinkin' this is done. We'll take it up later. The whelp won't always be around to save you from what you got comin'." Fingers tightened in bruising promise before he released her and stormed to the door. Hatred burned in the glare he sent Matthew before he clicked the lock. The door slammed back against the wall as he shoved it open, and it bounced back closed behind him as he stormed down the hallway.

She shut her eyes and let her head drop forward. Tremors raced through her body as she fought against a crashing wave of fear. A scream almost ripped lose as Matthew's boyish arms wrapped around her waist. Instead, she let out a squeak before forcing herself to relax.

"You all right, I'sa?" His use of the name he'd called her since he first learned to talk eased her.

Eliza managed a smile and wrapped her arms around his thin shoulders, hugging him tight. "I am now you're here. Thank you. Come on. I want to get out of this room."

At the door Matthew held her back, leaning out to make sure Silas wasn't in the hall before he led her out. They hurried upstairs to the school room.

Eliza sighed when the door closed behind them, but Matthew wasn't done. He grabbed a chair and shoved it under the knob. The action was like releasing a cork to the tension that had kept her going. She barely made it to a chair before her legs gave out. She didn't even realize she was crying until Matthew pressed his handkerchief into her hands and wrapped his arms around her neck.

"Oh, Matthew. I can't stay here. Not any longer. Silas is right. You can't be with me all the time. He might not dare do anything to you, but it's only a matter of time before he catches me alone."

"But you can't leave. Where would you go?" Tears

filled his eyes.

"Out west. I'll get a job."

"A job!" he burst out. "You can't. Mama needs you here. It's not right. And, what about me?"

"I don't want to leave you, but I can't stay here. Do you understand?"

He brushed at the tears on his face and nodded. "How would you even find a job?" He sniffled.

Eliza pulled him into her lap hugging him tight then easing him back. "Look at this." She reached into her apron pocket and drew out a paper folded into a small square. It crackled when she opened it. Her fingers trembled slightly as she held it out for her brother to read.

"I'sa, are you really going?"

Eliza had found the advertisement a week earlier and had been packing it with her since, trying to decide about taking the risk. Well, the risk was greater if she stayed. "Yes." She bit her bottom lip.

"But that's a long ways away. How can you?" He dropped his eyes back to the paper. "I'sa, a job?"

Eliza followed his gaze back to the advertisement for waitresses at train stations. The women must be women of strong moral character, from good families.

"This doesn't say where you'd be."

"I'm sure I'd get some say but, at least, it would be away. They assure clean, safe living conditions. I've asked around and been assured the claims are truthful."

"All right, I'll come with you, then you won't be alone."

"Oh Matthew." She smiled down, her eyes watering. "Thank you, but I'm afraid you can't. They only provide room and board for one, and you have to stay with your mother. She needs you to watch after her."

"How could she marry Mr. Marsh? Why can't she see what he's like?" His voice raised with frustration.

"I think she does. There's just nothing she can do now

they are married. I don't think she knew what kind of a man he was when she married him. Your Mama is a good, gentle woman. She looks for the good in others and our father was that kind of a man. I'm sure she must've presumed Mr. Marsh would be a good man, too. He put on those airs."

"He didn't fool me, and you didn't like him either."

"Yes, but she thought we were clinging to the memories of Papa. She was afraid to be alone." Just mentioning her father made the image of him come to her mind. He'd been a handsome, honorable man, quick to laugh and full of love for them.

"I'll miss you." Matthew pulled her thoughts back.

"I'll miss you too, but I'll write when I get settled. I'll send the post to Mrs. Harris next door. She won't tell Mr. Marsh."

"She doesn't like him either." There was a knowing quality in his voice.

"Yes, and I'll bet she'll have cookies for you when you go over."

His chin quivered. "I still don't want you to go."

"I know, I don't want to leave you either, but I can't stay here or Silas will hurt me. He'll do something very bad."

Her brother nodded with a face too grim for his young years. "I won't tell where you are. No matter what. I won't tell Mama either."

A wave of panic hit her at her brother's words. It might be safer if he didn't know but what if Silas did beat him. He hadn't raised a hand to him before, but his displeasure seemed to be growing stronger each day. Still, she didn't want to think of her brother hurt.

"Matthew, if you have to, if he ever hurts you, I want you to come to me. Tell Mrs. Harris, ask if she can buy you a ticket. Tell her I'll find a way to repay her."

"I have money, but maybe you better take it."

"No, love. I'll be fine. I have plenty to cover what I need until I start getting paid."

"A job. I don't think Mama would approve."

"She'll understand. It's what I have to do."

"I wish Papa was here." Tears flooded in his eyes.

Eliza pulled him tight. "I know, love." Feeling her own tears swell.

He buried his face into her shoulder.

"Just know he loved us and didn't want to leave us." She tilted her cheek down to lay against his head.

"It's not fair."

"I know, but accidents happen." She fought to calm the emotions ripping at her.

"I wish Mama had never married Mr. Marsh."

"So do I." She repeated the words under her breath.

He raised his head and looked up at her. "Do you think if we told Mama, we could all leave him?"

"I'm afraid not. Be brave now, for me and your Mama."

"But Eliza." Tears trickled down his cheeks. For a nine-year-old boy, he was so grown up, still he was just a little boy.

She wrapped him tightly in her arms and rocked back and forth as she'd done so often. Being almost ten years older, she'd always cared and watched over him, especially this last year after their father died. His mother had taken the loss hard. The coming of Silas Marsh into their home had added to the difficulties and strengthened their sibling bond.

That night Eliza stayed in her brother's room, not daring to chance leaving and being caught in her own. Silas had tried to order her down for supper, but Matthew had feigned being sick, forgoing the chance at dessert to make it viable.

Mrs. May, their cook, who never dared speak out but was very observant, smuggled them up a large dinner with dessert. Once Mathew fell asleep, Eliza settled down in the window seat that looked over the garden and wrote a letter to her stepmother.

She loved the woman who had become her mother when she so needed one at nine years old. Her own mother had died in child birth a year earlier leaving her father lonely with a young child to raise. She didn't want to worry her stepmother and hated to accuse Silas Marsh of his evilness, not wanting to hurt her. Eliza just hoped to ease her concern without giving too much information about what she had planned.

The house was long quiet when she finally snuck to her room and stuffed what belongings she dared take into a satchel then retrieved the little money she'd fretted away. Her footsteps barely made a whisper in the hall, but there were challenging creaks to avoid on the stairs. On the fourth step, Eliza came down on one spot that split the silence and made her pulse lurch. She froze, afraid any second a door would be thrown open and she'd be confronting Silas Marsh.

When it didn't happen, she continued down, slipping into the kitchen. By the light coming in through the windows, she quickly placed enough food in a bundle to last her for several days until she could hopefully get settled where they would send her.

A fissure of fear ran through her at the unknown only to be dampened down by the known. She couldn't stay here within Silas's reach. She couldn't bear the thought of what he would do if he ever got hold of her.

Opening the kitchen door, she stood staring out at the dark. With a glance over her shoulder, she brushed a tear from her cheek and stepped away from her home. The streets were filled with eerie shadows. Eliza became one more of them as she crept along.

It took nearly an hour to reach the train yard. The stillness in the air was as monstrous as the dark serpent like minions lined up behind the station. Unable to force her feet to move another step, she sank down on a stack of crates tucked against a building across the street from the office of the hiring agent. Exhaustion swept over her. A whimpered sigh escaped with some of her tension.

Eliza never figured she would sleep, but the next thing she knew, a wagon clattered by startling her awake. She straightened, looking out at the early morning. There were only a few men moving around, but by the time she stepped from the outhouse by the train station, the bustling had commenced on the streets. Washing up with water from the rain barrel helped to wipe away her lingering exhaustion

Her attempt to eat was quickly given up because she was far too jittery for any appetite to survive. Returning the food to the bag, she settled back to wait for the hiring agent to arrive. Nearly an hour passed before she saw a tidy bald man put a key in the lock and open the door.

Eliza stood and brushed her hands down her drab, gray skirt that was her mourning outfit from her father's death. Even though the time of bereavement had ended, she figured it was fitting to wear it now because it was the death of her life here. Also, it worked because she didn't want to draw attention to herself and figured it was as plain and bland as could be.

She'd gotten good at playing down her appearance. She knew men found her beautiful but didn't think it would help her get a position. Still, she definitely didn't want to look slovenly. With the dust and wrinkles brushed out the best she could, Eliza took a deep breath to strengthen her resolve and crossed to the building.

If the man refused to hire her, she didn't know what she'd do. She couldn't go home. That was certain. But what options were there for her if she was turned away? Eliza didn't want to consider the possibility farther, it was not an option. She had to get the job. Her resolve firmly in place, she stepped up onto the boardwalk.

The door stood open to let the spring air in. The man, who she'd seen enter, stood with his back to the door, thumbing through the top drawer of the file cabinet. The light through the window glistened off his bald head. He was shorter than her by several inches. Far from a menacing looking man but he held her life in his hands.

"Excuse me." Her voice cracked under the tension and she swallowed as he turned. His face was reassuringly kind.

"May I help you?"

"Yes, sir. I saw the advertisement about the openings for work in rail stations. I was wondering if there were any positions still available."

The man looked her up and down, then motioned her to a chair. "Please have a seat. We do have openings available but I must ask you several questions. The first being your name."

"Oh, yes. Sorry. Eliza." She reached out her hand to shake. "Eliza Telford." She gave her mother's maiden name, not totally sure why. She watched as he wrote it down.

"I presume it is miss?"

"Yes."

"Would you mind telling me why you wish this post? You said you read the advertisement, so you know you will be required to leave your home and family for the length of your employment and travel out west."

"My father died. My mother remarried and I am no longer welcome at home. I need to make my own life. The paper says that it will be a safe and respectable place to work. I have asked around and was able to talk to several gentlemen in my neighborhood who had traveled and stopped at station houses and have confirmed the claims."

"What is your work experience?"

"I have none except what I've had at home, but I am a hard worker. I am not afraid to work and I am a good cook."

The man smiled. "All right. When would you like to start?"

"Immediately. I have nowhere to go." As soon as she spoke, she worried it was the wrong thing to say.

The man's head jerked up and he stared at her, eyes narrowing slightly.

A fissure of fear filled her until a look of concern crossed his face.

"Just a minute." He stood and went to the cabinet, opening one of the draws. After a moment, he pulled out several pages and looked them over. "We do have immediate openings in one of our new Colorado locations. The place has only been operating for less than a month. If you're willing to go to Colorado."

"I'm willing." Relief left her weak.

"I haven't told you anything about it. It's a new establishment for us, so there will be extra work getting it running smoothly. A lot will be expected of you."

"That's no problem," she assured him.

"The community is pretty settled. Ranching, mining and there is some vacationing that is starting up, but I can assure you it is respectable. The women there will be in similar circumstances as you. Many orphans, or from families that can't afford so many to keep."

He looked her over as if that might make her change her mind, but that wasn't going to happen. She'd go any place that would get her out of Silas Marsh's reach. "That's fine."

"You certain?"

"Yes, sir."

"We haven't discussed wages and terms." He raised an eyebrow.

"It was quite clear in the advertisement, or is that not correct."

"No, it is correct. The company pays the ticket there, and will provide room and board. You are paid your wages at the end of each month. If you work six months your return ticket will be covered or you can go anywhere you choose. If you leave before six months, your wages will be forfeited, as will further passage."

Eliza managed a nod. Six months seemed like such a long time if she didn't like it there but, then again, what choice did she have? "I understand."

"All right." He shifted some more papers. "I will need you to fill this out and I will go see to your passage." He pulled a pocket watch form his vest and glanced at it. "We should be able to have you on the nine-fifteen train, if that is acceptable? You said you are ready to leave."

"Yes. I've already said my farewells."

"Very well then. You can start on that and I will be right back if you have any questions."

Excitement and fear warred within her as Eliza looked down at the papers on the blotter in front of her.

Two hours later, the war was still raging inside of her as the city fell behind. A tear escaped. Eliza sighed as she squeezed her eyes shut. She was alone, but she was safe.

A shudder passed through her and she began to shake. Her stomach clenched and for a moment she thought she would be sick. Biting her lip, she managed to keep in the sobs that wanted to escape.

Eliza tilted her head back and fought for composure. It was all right. She could do this. She really could do this. She just had to remain positive. She wouldn't be alone. There would be a lot of other young ladies there. The main thing, Silas Marsh would no longer be a factor in her life.

Forcing the thoughts from her mind Eliza stared out the window watching the countryside pass by. Soon her head started to bob as weariness overtook her. She dozed most of the morning away, only to be jarred awake by the conductor announcing they were coming into the station where she'd have to change trains to the one she'd be on all the way to Colorado. She'd only have fifteen minutes there before the other train would be pulling out.

It was a good thing she'd brought her own food. There wouldn't be time to get any. Not that she wanted to spend any of the money she had on that. She might have assured Matthew she had enough to assuage his concerns but, in all honesty, she didn't have much. Still, she'd get by if she was frugal. She'd be okay.

The train slowed. Glancing out the window, Eliza could see they were nearing the station. The town stretched out from the tracks. She watched people hurrying around. The scene was so familiar she could almost believe she was back where she'd boarded the train. Her throat went dry. She scanned faces, afraid she'd see Marsh among them. Of course that was foolish. She was a long way from home.

Anxious, Eliza stood to drag out her satchel just as the train lurched, throwing her into the edge of the seat. Pain spiked in her knee and hip, but she managed to catch hold of the back of the seat and stay upright.

The next instant, the aisle filled with people pouring out onto the platform. Eliza moved with the flow out the door. Stepping away from the crowd, she looked for the other train, but the tracks were all clear except for the train they'd come in on.

Panic choked her. She pulled out the note the hiring agent had given her, and reread the train number and the time. Surely, it couldn't refer to late at night.

Were they late arriving and the other train had already left? That couldn't be happening, could it?

Chapter Two

Eliza spun around until she spied a station employee and wove her way through the thinning mass to reach him. It was all she could do not to interrupt his conversation with another couple. She shifted from side to side, biting her bottom lip to keep from blurting out her fear.

When he finished and turned her way, his eyes widened in a common reaction to her looks. "I'm sorry to keep you waiting miss." He stumbled on the words. "May I be of assistance?"

"Yes, please. The train for Colorado. Have I missed it?"

"Why, no, miss." He pulled his watch from his pocket with well-practiced ease. "It should be arriving in eight minutes. Are you meeting someone?" There were obvious signs of interest in him.

"No, I'm supposed to be on it and thought I'd missed it. When the time was written, it must have been its arrival, not departure. I'm sorry I troubled you."

"No trouble, I'm here to help. You have almost forty minutes if you care to step in and get something to eat. We have excellent meals, served up promptly. The train leaves right on the hour. I'll be announcing a ten and a five minute warning to give everyone time to board."

"Thank you." Eliza pulled back allowing the next person waiting to take her place.

Eliza glanced at the building. It looked inviting

enough, but she knew she wouldn't be going inside. She had plenty of food and she wanted to save her money, but she was grateful for the opportunity to stretch her legs. She still felt a bit shaky from the thought of missing the train.

It only took a couple minutes to walk the full length of the platform, so she stepped down on the boardwalk. People rushed along it, paying her no mind. When she reached the end of the street she turned back. She'd only covered about half the distance when she heard the sound of an approaching train. She picked up her pace.

People streamed off the train, once more packing the platform. A large number moved into the restaurant. She stood back and watched. Surely there was no way that many people could be served a meal and make it back on the train that was to leave in thirty minutes.

As the entryway cleared, curiosity pulled her forward. Glancing in one of the windows, she was staggered by the size of the place. Tables covered with white linen filled the room. She was going to be working in a place like that. She'd be one of the women in black dresses and crisp white aprons hurrying through the room serving the patrons.

Eliza eased up behind a young woman standing in the open doorway to get a better view. Would the place she was going be this big? She didn't think so. This was a main city. Her stomach muscles tightened. She had no idea what it would be like out west.

Wanting to get a better view, she stepped up beside the woman who was peering through the door in much the same manner that she was. Eliza strained around the doorframe trying to take everything in without attracting attention. The woman turned abruptly right into her. They staggered apart, each catching their balance.

"Pardon me, miss," the woman said right on top of Eliza's, "Pardon me."

The woman, who was about her age with a mass of brown hair piled on her head, pulled back to let her pass.

"Oh, no." Eliza said. "I'm not going in. I just wanted to see. You're not going in either?" she asked when the woman stepped farther away from the entrance.

The woman looked through the door, longing evident in her soft green eyes, but she shook her head. "No, I'm just waiting for my train." She had a beautiful, warm voice that flowed like a melody that drew a person in. "I'm just stretching my legs. It's so hard on the train with its swaying." Her cheeks pinked, as if she'd said too much.

Eliza nodded. "I understand. I was sneaking a peek inside to see what it was like." It hit her that the other woman was doing the exact same thing. "I'm going to be working in a similar place in Colorado. At least, I presume it will be similar."

At the widening of the woman's eyes, Eliza knew she'd guessed right even before her words confirmed it.

"Me, too."

"I'm Eliza Telford." There was no pause in giving her name this time.

"Hannah James." Hannah glanced back at the building.

"Are you sure you don't want to go in? It's all right." She felt a touch of longing to enter the building, but quashed it. "I was just going to walk around until time to board."

"I was planning on walking myself. It gets kind of stifling on the train. I hope it isn't so packed."

"You came in on that train?"

Hannah nodded. "I barely made it on before it pulled out and the only place left was in the front of the first car. It was noisy. I'm hoping to move farther back."

"That's good to know. I was farther back but was so tired I probably wouldn't have noticed. You're not traveling with anyone?"

"No, I'm on my own. You, too?"

This time it was Eliza's turn to nod.

"Would you like to sit with me? I would love some

company and it sounds like we're going to the same place."

Relief flowed through Eliza at the hoped for offer. "Yes. Thank you. I was just bemoaning being lonely."

They'd almost reached the end of the train yard walk when Hannah glanced back over her shoulder. "Let's head back and find a place to sit."

They returned to the train at a much quicker pace. After a second to confer with the conductor as to where they were allowed to sit, and where he'd suggest, they settled in the fourth car and had just picked seats facing each other when the ten minute warning announcement rang out.

People trickled onto the train. When the five minute was called out, the car was only half full. Several more late comers bustled on, but there were seats enough that no one tried to squish in with them.

Facing the back, Eliza watched two men come through the door. Both were sharp faced with hardened glares that pulled a shiver from her. One had a wicked scar on his chin. They each seemed to scan the people on the train, one taking one side while the one with the scar focused on their side. His eyes tightened when they rested on Hannah.

Eliza looked at the open spot next to her and her throat tightened. Would they ask to join them or just force their way into the open seats? If they did, that would leave her and Hannah trapped between the men and the window.

The one with the scar nudged his partner and they headed forward, their chilling gazes locked on their row. Eliza's breath became painful as if she really was breathing in icy air. She reached for Hannah's hand just as an older woman pushed her way into their row.

"There you are dears. I was getting worried I wasn't going to make it and the train would leave without me," she said loudly.

As the men approached, the older woman shifted in a way Eliza could almost believe was on purpose, cutting off their view. When the woman frowned at the men from under her bonnet, Eliza realized it really had been intentional and it worked.

The men lost interest and hurried past, moving out the door into the next car.

Eliza let out the breath she'd been unconsciously holding and looked up at the woman. "Thank you."

"You are most welcome. I didn't like the looks of those two eyeing you sweet young ladies. I won't have it." She bristled. "I'm just back two rows with my husband. If you are in need of any more assistance, you just let me know."

"Thank you," Eliza said, Hannah's gratitude barely following.

The woman gave them a kind smile and moved back by her husband, barely making it into her seat before the train lurched and started its slow motion forward.

"That was nice of her," Hannah whispered, looking nervously in the direction the men disappeared. "Do you think they'll be back?"

"Hopefully not, but if they do, we'll take her up on her offer."

Hannah had gone pale.

"Are you okay?" Eliza leaned forward and squeezed her hand.

Hannah nodded.

"Oh," Eliza caught sight of the two men standing on the platform as the train rolled past picking up speed.

"What?" Panic made Hannah's voice break and she ducked down.

"The men aren't on the train. I saw them back there." Relief whooshed from her, echoed as Hannah sighed.

Eliza studied Hannah who worried her bottom lip with her teeth much the way she did when troubled. "Hannah, have you had any problems?"

The woman glanced out the window. "No, not on the

train."

Eliza was trying to figure out how, or if she dared ask more when Hannah beat her to it. "Have you had problems? You are very beautiful."

"Thank you." Eliza decided to take it as a compliment since there was no snootiness like she got from some women, still there seemed to be something Hannah wasn't saying. "Are you sure there isn't something wrong?" Eliza could have sworn she paled again, but she shook her head.

"No." Then softly, under her breath, Eliza thought she heard, "I hope not."

Hannah's gaze came back to meet hers, and Eliza felt she was meeting a kindred spirit. Whether Hannah felt the same she couldn't be certain, but as one, they reached for the other's hand.

A smile came to Hannah's face that Eliza returned.

"We're going to be all right," Eliza said confidently.

"Yes. We're going to be all right," Hannah agreed, then repeated it stronger.

The city fell away into rolling hills and grassland. They chatted about the trip and what they thought it might be like in Colorado. Both were looking forward to new lives, though they both avoided saying why they'd left their old ones.

Realizing she was hungry, Eliza pulled out her bag and dug inside for the food sack she'd packed. Hannah's eyes widened when she saw it, then she looked away, catching her lip once more between her teeth. Eliza remembered her expression back at the restaurant and put the looks she'd seen together – hunger.

"Would you like to join me?"

Hannah jerked back, a stunned expression evident on her face. "I – I wouldn't want to take your food." The longing in her eyes belied the words.

"I have plenty for the trip. I wasn't sure how long it would take so I packed extra." She smiled. "Besides, you would share with me in reverse." That won, Hannah smiled and nodded.

Eliza handed her one of her thick pieces of bread.

Hannah bit in and actually sighed, closing her eyes as she chewed.

"When was the last time you ate?"

Hannah opened her eyes, swallowed and blushed. "Noon meal … yesterday."

"Hannah! Why didn't you tell me sooner? You're starving." Eliza opened her bag wide. "What would you like?"

Hannah met her eyes, her lips twitched, and it was suddenly like all the tension escaped and she started to laugh, a beautiful sound, that brought lightness back into Eliza's heart and she joined in.

"Friends," Eliza got out as she tried to get herself back under control, aware people around them were staring.

"Always," Hannah agreed, and they settled back to eat.

The future didn't feel quite so daunting now she wasn't facing it totally alone.

Chapter Three

"Well, aren't you a pretty thing?" The nasally-toned words grated on Eliza's nerves, but she ignored the comment as she set the basket of bread on the table and filled water glasses. After nearly a month on the job, she was getting used to the comments.

"Heck, Floyd, something wrong with you? That ain't pretty, that's right beautiful. I've never seen a woman to compare. Give us a smile sweetheart."

Eliza fought to keep her shivers from making her hand tremble. After four weeks, she figured she should be good at ignoring such remarks, but every once in a while someone disturbed her, and these men fit in that category. She hadn't seen any of the three men at the table before and unfortunately the last train of the day had already pulled out, so that meant they wouldn't be hurrying to leave.

"If you'll excuse me." She kept her voice neutral as she tried to shift away.

"Now, don't go scurrying off." One reached for her hand. Luckily, she was able to pull back before he caught it.

"Excuse me." She stepped back out of reach of the next man. "I have a lot of other people to serve." She was grateful for the convenient excuse. Unfortunately, with no train leaving, it didn't carry much urgency.

"We don't have to go anywhere. Bless our lucky stars, this is our stopping point."

"But others are waiting. Now, if you'll pardon me." Eliza positioned her tray in between her and the offending man and moved out of his reach. She was still conscious of the man's eyes on her as she placed plates on the next table. Her heart was full of dread at the thought of having to return and deal with the men.

She jumped when a hand came down on her arm and bit back a cry. Swinging around, she found herself looking into a pair of warm green eyes. "Hannah," she sighed in relief, almost collapsing back on the table.

"Sorry," Hannah apologized. "Why don't you trade tables with me."

Eliza knew she should decline the offer that put her friend in the reach of the unruly men, but was too relieved to refuse. "Are you certain?" she whispered back.

"Yes, I can handle them." Her no-nonsense, confident way was one of the things Eliza liked and admired about her.

Eliza gave her a grateful smile, took the basket of rolls Hannah carried, and turned to the next table to place the basket in the center. "What may I get for you?" she asked before glancing up. "For our specials today, we have roast beef or chicken with potatoes and green beans or beef stew. For dessert we have apple pie, peach cobbler or rich butter cake."

She looked up into the eyes of the man across the table and forgot all else.

Eyes gray as steel looked at her, but there was no coldness or the lusty heat she'd experienced all too often. They did appear to be interested, but his gaze was locked in intelligence, so she couldn't be certain. He was clean shaven, dressed neatly but not in a dandy fashion. There was something that was a touch rugged about him. He was a man not to be swayed.

A smile crested his lips, but the friendly type. "I'll have the roast beef, peach cobbler with a portion of sweet cream on it, if you have it."

It was a second before she could get her mind around the words as it wanted to cling to the soft baritone sound of his voice.

"Yes, sir." What was happening to her? She'd never reacted to a man like this before. Eliza forced her mind to clear and turned to the other three at the table. "Gentlemen?"

The next was the exact same, then roast beef with pie, and the last chicken with pie. With the requests firmly in her mind, Eliza hurried away careful to circumvent the table with the men who had hassled her.

She was gathering the food at the counter when another woman pressed against her side, ramming her hip painfully up against the edge. Thinking it was an accident, Eliza eased aside to give her room to reach whatever she was after.

Instead of going for something, the woman leaned in. "I saw what you did. Changing tables to get to Cord Bartlett." Bessie, Eliza's least favorite person there, hissed in her ear. "I'm telling you now. Don't be thinking about him, he's mine."

Eliza glanced up and had to suppress a frown. Before she could form a verbal response, Bessie bumped into her again to add emphasis as she moved away. Eliza sighed glancing back at Bessie. The woman was way off. She glanced at the table she'd just come from before turning back to her task. *Could he be courting Bessie?*

Bessie was pretty enough. Several inches shorter than her, which made her average height. Brown hair with pale skin, which she pampered excessively. Her eyes would be a lovely dark brown if she wasn't always glaring and wrinkling her petite nose up.

Eliza shrugged again, adding a gravy boat to her tray. She'd heard Bessie had her sights on the banker, and she'd seen her playing up to the sheriff whenever he came in, along with several other men in town. Basically, any good-looking man, and a few not so good-looking if they had a lot of money.

Eliza stifled the impulse to turn and look at the man again. She didn't need to. He definitely fit the bill of good-looking. He, in fact, was incredibly handsome. That didn't matter though, she was not there to find a man.

Eliza set her mind on loading the tray. The train rush might be over and the people here now were either locals or staying on, still, there was a standard of fast, efficient service to up hold along with quality food. She didn't want to risk a tongue lashing by the supervisor, Mrs. Hyde. Not that she needed a reason. The woman had taken an immediate dislike of her and looked for any excuse to berate her.

She'd never forget how, when she first arrived, the woman had looked her up and down with a scowl creasing her brow. "What were they thinking? How am I ever to find a suitable uniform for you at your odd height?" Then her lip curled. "Don't think your looks will gain you any special treatment. You will work just like any of the other girls." Eliza had worked hard, harder than most, but nothing was ever enough to please Lenore Hyde.

Mrs. Hyde was always there watching, ready to speak her daily quota of chastisement, as if Eliza was going to forget. "You are not here to find a husband. You are not to socialize with customers."

Eliza placed the last plate on her tray then wove her way back to the table. The men were discussing cattle when she approached. Trying not to interrupt their conversation, she slid the meals in front of them.

They all fell silent and stared at her.

"Thank you," the man who'd caught her interest said softly as she placed his meal in front of him.

"You're welcome." She managed to get out as her heartbeat kicked up. "I'll be watching when to bring your dessert, but if you need anything else, just let me know."

He tipped his head in acknowledgement.

Eliza scurried away to prepare dessert and refill water and coffee at her other occupied table.

CRED

Though he tried not to be obvious about it, Cord Bartlett couldn't help but watch the woman as she crossed the room. No matter her poorly fit uniform, the tightness of the hair knotted on top of her head, or the way she tipped down her face, there was no hiding the fact that she was a stunningly, beautiful woman. Maybe the most beautiful he'd ever seen. Not that it said what she was truly like, but it was hard not to take notice.

Her height might attract some men, put off others, but for him, as a man at six feet three inches tall, he found it very appealing, but what he found most attractive were the glimpses of blue eyes the color of springtime skies.

A man would risk any challenge or make a fool of himself just to have them focused on him. Well, he wasn't in for making himself a fool by one of these women who traveled out here to catch a husband where they figured the pickin's were good.

He actually couldn't fault the women. There was wisdom in it, and they surely did need women out here. But, he'd just spent the last couple years putting all his efforts, working like a dog, to get his ranch the way he wanted it, and there was still too much to do to get side-tracked by a woman.

Maybe in a year he'd think about finding himself a wife. He shifted his attention back to the conversation. The business had all been solidified, the contracts signed, but the enthusiasm had yet to wane. It was going to be mutually profitable for all. Even better for him than he'd hoped.

He was aware of the woman coming up behind him. He didn't even have to look to know it was her. Instead of stopping at their table, she went to the next one over, serving it. He wasn't surprised when she actually came into view. Odd, there were easily a dozen women serving, all identically clad, but he hadn't noticed any of them. But after five minutes, he could tell exactly where she was as if she was locked into his mind.

He concentrated on the excellent meal. Since the opening, the establishment had quickly become known for its quality of food and reasonable prices. The locals had learned to avoid the place during train stopovers, when it was a bustle of activity, trying to serve all those who only had a short time for a decent meal before they had to be on their way.

In between and after those times, it was a touch more relaxed and elegant fare. It had been a few weeks since he'd been in here. She must be new because he would have remembered her. His thoughts started to slip right back to her even before she stopped at the table to refill their water, coffee cups, and Samuel's tea.

"I'll have your dessert right out to you." Her soft voice skimmed across his senses putting them on high alert. If he'd been out on the range, he'd been looking for trouble. A second later, when she leaned in to take his plate and replace it with a dish laden with a large portion of cobbler liberally doused with sweet cream and her hand brushed his as he reached for his spoon, he knew he was in trouble. Current shot up his arm. The only satisfying thing was her reaction.

She jerked her hand back. Her eyes went wide, flashing a stunning blue, as they met his. Her beautiful, soft pink mouth was open in a perfect little O. She looked innocent and tempting at once, then her chin tipped down and away.

"Pardon me." She fled from the table, but not before he caught sight of the rosy glow tinting her cheeks.

It took effort not to shake his head. Could that have been right? Could a woman, so incredibly beautiful, blush at just a brush of a hand? He found the notion intriguing. He'd taken three bites of the cobbler before the wonderful flavor of it registered. He sighed with contentment. The dessert was as exceptional as the whole meal had been.

He'd have to start thinking of meals soon. No, what he needed was to start looking for a new housekeeper now that Mrs. Denton had let him know she was moving to California at the end of the month, to live with her daughter's family. He didn't have time to keep house, fix meals and run a ranch the size of his. Besides, he couldn't tolerate his own cooking. He could eat with the hands like he had before Mrs. Denton, but he'd gotten used to the big house always being clean and his clothes laundered.

Out of the corner of his eye, he caught the swish of a black skirt held tight to the waist with a starched, stark-white apron. He didn't need to raise his gaze to know which waitress it was. She placed dishes around the next table over, then turned to retrieve the two empty pie plates from his associates before heading back to the counter.

"Hey where'd you go?" The words came loud and irritated from behind him. "You been avoiding us?" There was no missing the annoyance in the tone.

"Someone else is handling your table." The soft voice he recognized as the beautiful blonde, held forced politeness.

"But we want you."

"I'm sorry but I have other assignments. If you please, I need to get back to my duties." Unease filled the words.

"Don't go." The man snapped.

"We just want some of your time." Another lower voice followed.

"Please, let me go!" This time the words came with panic and had Cord standing before the shattering of the plates she dropped, jerked everyone's attention around.

She leaned back from the man that crowded into her and was blocked by another man standing behind her. Her blue eyes were wide again, this time with fear.

Fury roared through Cord at the sight of rough, tanned fingers banded around her delicate wrist.

"Please." Her cry came again.

"Release her." Cord kept his voice low, stressing every syllable.

"This doesn't concern ..." The man standing behind her broke off as he looked up. Cord had him by a full head in height. In fact, neither man was much taller than her, but they had her by at least thirty or forty pounds. Both thick built, closer to his weight.

Another man at the table stood. "You don't want to get involved in this. We're just talking to the lady here."

"The lady has made it clear she doesn't wish to talk to you. She's trying to do her job. Release her and let her get back to it."

"You tellin' us what to do?" The one holding her arm finally released it as he turned to him.

"I am. It's time for you to leave. Pay the money you owe for the food and dishes you broke and get out." Cord met him glare for glare.

"Come on, Huck." The last to stand glanced around the room, then dropped his hand on Huck's arm. "Let's get out of here. We don't need trouble."

Huck's brows tightened. He glanced back at the beauty then back up at Cord. His lips pinched in clear debate, then he turned and strode out. The other two men dropped some money on the table and hurried after him.

"Eliza, are you all right?"

Cord hadn't noticed the other woman come up, but now she stepped forward sliding an arm around the beauty, Eliza. The name ran over in his mind. He liked it.

"Yes." The answer squeaked from her and her whole body visibly tremble.

Another, older woman came bustling over, but when she opened her mouth the words came out scathing. "Get this mess cleaned up and back to work. And those dishes will be coming out of your wages." The woman, who was clearly the supervisor, hissed quietly so the words wouldn't carry past the women. Only standing so close allowed him to hear.

The words rankled Cord. She hadn't done anything to deserve the remark. He glanced at the money on the table. "It looks like they left enough to cover the damages, but if not, I'll cover the rest."

The woman huffed and stomped away in not much less of a temper than the men had. Cord knew she couldn't argue with him and hoped that would end the incident.

The blue eyes came up to him again. "That's not necessary," she said softly. "Thank you for your assistance."

"My pleasure." He tipped his head. "Are you all right?"

"Yes, thanks to you." She met his gaze a moment before glancing away.

"Here let me help you clean this up." The other woman said. She was average height with brown hair and eyes, pretty but nothing compared to Eliza. Cord recognized her for what she was immediately, the quiet, hard-working type that got things done in the background without calling attention to herself. The only reason she was there now was in support of her friend.

"I can get it." Eliza said.

"Nonsense, I'll take care of this. You finish clearing their plates." Without waiting, she squatted down to pick up pieces of the plates.

"Thanks, Hannah." Eliza turned back to him. "I'll just get those dishes." She picked up her tray and eased around him to clear the table.

Cord noticed the other men at his table had risen also, they returned to their seats as he sat down. He was aware of several glances she sent his way and the faint blush that colored her cheeks.

"Thank you, again." She looked at the others with him. "Gentlemen, I hope you have a good day," she said, then left, disappearing back into the kitchen.

"That is one beautiful woman. Must be hard on her working in a place like this where unwanted attention is put her way. Well done on you, Cord," Henry said.

"Yes, very. You didn't even need our assistance. I hope they'll keep going, right out of town. Otherwise you made yourself some enemies."

The words dug deep in his soul. He wasn't worried about himself, but what about Eliza? The station houses were known as safe, respectable places, but what if the men hung around town? What if they came after her again? The notion didn't sit well with him at all.

୦୫୨୦

Eliza slid the tray onto the counter and quickly unloaded the dishes. Her heart still pounded, but she couldn't quite say if it was from the men or from her rescuer. She blew out a breath. Closing her eyes only brought his image to her mind. Since her father died, she hadn't had a man stand up for her except for her brother, and Matthew wasn't quite a man. Definitely not a man like her rescuer.

Shaking Mr. Bartlett from her thoughts, she turned just as a half-full gravy boat was shoved against her chest, coating the front if her pristine white apron in brown goop.

"Clumsy, aren't you today," Bessie said with a touch of glee, dispelling any thoughts that it might have been an accident. "I told you, stay away from Cord Bartlett." Venom poured from the woman before she glanced over her shoulder.

"Oh, Eliza." Amelia came rushing over before Eliza could do anything but sigh. "Here." Amelia grabbed a towel and started to clean it up, only making a bigger mess.

"What is this?" Mrs. Hyde, the supervisor's shriek

made them both jump. "Get on a clean apron and get back to work and make sure that's taken to be laundered tonight." She hit the last word with emphasis then sent a scathing look at Amelia.

The only person Mrs. Hyde seemed to have more contempt for than her was Amelia. Eliza didn't even think that it was because Amelia had obviously never done any work before, Amelia tried hard and was willing to learn. No, Eliza figured it was because Amelia was petite and very pretty with thick black hair and green eyes that sparkled, now that they had lost the guardedness they'd held her first two weeks there.

With nothing else to do about it, Eliza went in back to rinse her apron, add it to the laundry and retrieve her spare one.

Chapter Four

Eliza sighed in relief when the last customer left that evening, not that their work was done, but it had been an exhausting day. To top it off, she had to help with the main room cleaning and set-up for morning. Fortunately, she was with Hannah and LuAnn, who was one of the most pleasant women and a good worker. There should have been a fourth but Arlene was not feeling well, and Mrs. Hyde actually let her go upstairs to lay down since the others agreed that it was all right with them that she did so.

LuAnn called goodnight, picked up the stack of trays and headed into the kitchen.

A couple minutes later, Eliza squared up the last chair to the linen draped table, directly in front of the china place setting and followed Hannah to the kitchen.

"Quite a day." Hannah waited at the door for her. "I hope those men never come back."

Eliza suppressed a shudder, not having to ask who she was referring to. She was about to answer when Hannah pushed the door open revealing Amelia on her knees, cleaning the floor. The dainty woman put all her strength into the motion.

"Amelia," Eliza looked around and saw no one else. "What are you doing?"

Amelia sat back and brushed a lock of dark hair back from her face. "Mrs. Hyde said I left too much water standing on the floor when I mopped it and insisted that I do it again with a rag so I could learn to do it right."

Eliza shook her head. Others got away with stuff all time, especially Mrs. Hyde's favorites, but her and Amelia never would. Eliza knew her height and looks accounted for some of what prickled the woman, how those affected her job she didn't know.

With Amelia, besides being a delicate beauty, she had a total lack of knowledge how to do the simplest chore, from washing dishes, to sweeping, or preparing food. The only thing she seemed proficient at was polishing silver. When she first arrived it set her up for berating from Mrs. Hyde. But Amelia learned fast, usually just needing to be shown once.

The problem was Mrs. Hyde made it hard for anyone to teach her. Most of the others avoided her to escape the overseer's wrath. How Mrs. Hyde acted didn't dissuaded Eliza, she didn't care because she was already despised by the woman.

Hannah was too kind not to help, and since she was too competent to find fault with, she got away with helping Amelia. Not that Hannah cared what Mrs. Hyde thought. The three had become fast friends from the moment they took Amelia under their wing.

Looking around the room, Eliza suspected the floor had been done right. She certainly didn't see any standing water left.

"Where is everyone else?" Eliza asked.

"They finished."

"What about the pots and pans?" Hannah asked, looking across the kitchen at the pile stacked there.

Eliza wasn't at all surprised when Amelia's answer came.

"To reinforce that I learn to do my work right, I'm to finish them.

Eliza could guess that meant one of Mrs. Hyde's favorites was on pans for the night. It wasn't the first time the woman did something like that. In fact, Eliza could probably narrow it to four girls, but didn't take time to check with one and reached for a rag.

Hannah was already crossing to the pans.

"Hannah, you've already done your work," Amelia objected when Hannah picked up the kettle of hot water and added some to the wash pan.

"And you've done yours," Hannah replied calmly.

Eliza knelt on the floor on the opposite side of the room and started to wipe. "What are you going to do with your free day tomorrow?" she asked Hannah.

"I really don't have much to do, since our first payday isn't for four more days. It's hard to believe we've been here a month. I guess I'll go for a walk, maybe sit and read. Hettie said I could borrow her book."

"That sounds wonderful." Amelia sighed. She'd only been there three weeks and had yet to have a free day because Mrs. Hyde insisted she use her supposed-to-be free day for training. "I wish we could have our free day together."

"Unfortunately, that is not likely." Eliza moved forward, rubbing the floor in large semi circles. Mrs. Hyde will keep it from happening."

Amelia nodded in agreement.

Eliza had had only one free day, and at the last minute Mrs. Hyde moved it up two days, to a day that started out overcast and ended up rainy. It wasn't that she had anything planned but resting and writing Matthew, but it was the irritation of Mrs. Hyde's pettiness to do that to her. Especially since there was nothing to fault in her work.

She and Hannah were two of the best workers there. Five more months, then she could either move somewhere else or find a new job. No, she'd have to look into going to another station. The only problem was, could all three of them change to the same location? She really hated to leave them. For the first time in her life, she felt like she had true friends.

She looked at the other two women. They couldn't be more different, but in the short time, they'd become so close. More like the sisters she'd never had – any of them ever had. "Have you thought what you'll do when our post here is up?"

Both Hannah and Amelia stopped in mid-motion at her question.

"I actually like the town and the area." Hannah said obviously having the same thought Eliza had.

"I don't want to lose you as friends. I've never had real friends before." Amelia hit the other point going through her mind.

"We could ask for posts at the same station," Eliza ventured out. "Maybe one of the other Colorado ones."

They all exchanged smiles.

"I agree," Hannah said.

Amelia nodded. "I don't think I can continue on under Mrs. Hyde. I wonder if I can survive five months." She sighed.

"Well, at least you'll know how to do everything perfectly." Hannah's ever positive attitude was followed by a grin that brought a light-hearted feel to the air.

Eliza made one last swipe over the floor with her rag then tossed it at Hannah, who laughed and sidestepped. "I'd say we're done." Eliza climbed to her feet.

Amelia blew out a breath. "I'm so exhausted. Maybe I'll sleep down here. It'd save me from having to make it up the stairs."

"I'll get you up them." Hannah placed the last pot on the pile to dry, wiped down the wash area, then stepped in the storage room to put away the soiled cloths. "Oh, no!"

"What is it?" Eliza moved up behind her to look over her shoulder. There was no mistaking who the apron laid out on the floor belonged to, even without the large gravy stain. The extra almost foot length was a dead giveaway.

"Bessie was on laundry tonight," Amelia confirmed what Eliza could've guessed.

As if on cue, Bessie and another woman, Rebecca, who was slightly older entered.

Hannah turned on Bessie. "You forgot an apron."

"What?" The shock on her face was obviously not sincere. Bessie came up beside them and looked in the room. "You must have not put it in the pile in time. That's your responsibility." She smirked.

"I put it in the pile right after you spilled the gravy on it. You watched me do it."

"Well, at least you have one spare you can wear tomorrow." Bessie flounced away.

Eliza could almost hear the words flow from her, if you can go without getting it spilt on, and guessed she'd be lucky to make it through the morning without something happening.

Rebecca stepped forward. "That was not there when I helped gather the laundry. I saw it in the basket. I'll take it over."

Eliza smiled at the offer. "No, it's not necessary. I could use a peaceful walk tonight but thanks."

"I'll go with you." Hannah volunteered.

"It's okay. I won't be gone long." She picked up the apron and headed out the door.

Most of the town was closed up for the night. Peaceful, but for some noise coming from one of the saloons. The stars were already out. Eliza loved the evenings here. It had a totally different feeling than her home.

It only took a couple minutes to reach the laundress' house by taking the shortcut behind the buildings. She breathed in deep, letting the smell of honeysuckle growing nearby fill her.

She'd really hate to leave here when the time came. She wished there were other jobs in the area that didn't involve riding a horse or digging in a mine. Which besides the fact she'd never ridden a horse before, you had to be a man to do.

"What have we here?"

Eliza spun, recognizing the voice of Huck, the man who'd harassed her earlier that day. He didn't look any more pleasant. In fact, he looked like he'd been drinking heavily.

"We hit the mother lode tonight."

Eliza caught the movements of the other two men coming up on either side of her, trapping her between them.

"Have you ever seen anything so pretty?" Huck continued talking, drawing her attention, though she tried to watch them all at once and think. "Why don't you let down all that white-gold hair of yours, and let us have a look. I bet it's right fine."

Eliza backed up from the hand that reached toward her hair, only to have her way blocked.

"Now you don't want to be leaving." The look Huck gave her was a mirror image of the way Silas looked at her but with maybe a bit more cruelty.

"If you'll excuse me, I really have to get back." Her voice trembled though she fought against it. She took a breath to steady herself and caught a strong whiff of alcohol and sweat. "My shift starts early." Eliza jumped when a hand touched her elbow.

She struck out knocking it away, eliciting a harsh laugh.

"You're the prrr-ettiest thing I ever did see," the young man said. Floyd. His name popped in her mind as he reached again for her.

She jerked her arm away and hit him.

"Now that's not being very friendly." Huck, who was definitely the leader, took over.

"Leave me alone."

"We're just trying to be friendly, after all the trouble you caused us this afternoon, you owe us." His tone turned coarse on the last couple of words.

Eliza spun, jabbing out with her elbow, catching the closest man in the stomach then pushed Floyd away as she tried to break through."

⚇⚇

Cord didn't know why he was still in town. He could've easily made it home before dark. Just when he went to leave an unsettling feeling had come over him and he couldn't go.

He was on his second trip through town. On his first, there had been enough light to see into the station restaurant. There had been no difficulty recognizing Eliza with her friend Hannah setting the tables. The women worked long hours, but didn't everyone, he reflected.

If he was honest with himself, he had to admit part of the reason he was still in town was the woman. He hoped to get another look at her. She was a beautiful woman, no doubt about that, but there was more to her.

It was her eyes. If he wasn't a man who believed in making your own fate, he would say he'd just met his. And truth be told, he didn't think he'd complain too much. A man could get happily lost in those eyes.

He glanced at the station. It was all dark now, and only a couple lights shown in the women's dormitory above. It was time he got his horse and headed for home. At least there was enough moonlight that the trail wouldn't be hard to follow.

Cord stepped into the street and caught movement on the other side, then the sheriff and his friend stepped out of the shadows.

"You're in town late," Cal Steadman said in way of a greeting.

Cord shrugged. "Had a meeting."

"Heard there was some trouble at the station while I was out at the Benson's. Thanks for handling it."

"No problem. Knuckle-heads causing problems for one

of the waitresses." His stomach clenched at the thought.

"Which one?"

If Cord didn't miss his guess, there was interest in the man's voice beyond being the sheriff. Though, what man wouldn't be interested?

"I caught her name – Eliza I think." He liked the sound of it on his lips.

Cal's interest seemed to ease, and he nodded. "She's a beautiful woman and real nice. Someone ought to marry her and put all the rest of the fools out of their misery."

"You interested?" Cord felt his hackles raise again.

"Not me." He shook his head. "Just saying."

The tightness that had crept up on him eased. "Well, I best be headed for home."

"Yeah, I'm just makin' a last walk through of the town then headin' in. Luckily it looks like a quiet night."

They nodded to each other but split going their opposite ways. Cal, the way he'd just come, and Cord continued to where he usually left his horse. He was just passing by the alley that led behind the general store when he heard a small cry. His first thought was a cat, but unease had him stopping to listen.

"Leave me alone!"

The cry came just as he took another step. Eliza! He spun, certain it was her.

Chapter Five

He broke into a run, the rumble of men's voices drawing him back behind the building.

A grunt followed immediately by a sharp cry which was cut off into a squeak, had him lengthening his stride.

"A wild cat. We're gonna have fun with you."

The words ignited fire in his veins. The sight of Eliza held trapped between three men fueled it to an inferno.

Eliza's arms were pinned to her side. One man, Floyd he remembered, had a filthy hand over her mouth. She whimpered and struggled to break free, stamping her foot down on the foot of one of the men. It didn't seem to have much effect, but she kept their focus from him as he covered the distance.

Cord reached them, grabbing the first man by his collar. He jerked him around and slammed his fist into the man's face. Huck. He barely registered his identity from earlier before dropping him and turning to the next, the biggest of the men. They were probably equal in weight but the man was a couple inches shorter. The man was already sending a meaty fist at him.

Cord got his arm up to deflect the blow, sidestepped, and thrust out his own strike that caught the man solidly in the jaw, hardly staggering him. The fist he plowed into his middle wasn't any more successful, producing only a faint grunt.

Cord barely saw the round-house coming. He ducked

the fist that would've likely taken his head off, or at the least, left him laid out on the ground unconscious and no help to Eliza. Anger surged through his body fueling his next strike, an uppercut that caught the man right under the chin. The big man's head snapped up as he toppled over backward.

Again not waiting, Cord turned in time to see Floyd toss Eliza to the side. She hit into the side of the building and crumpled to the ground.

Instinct had Cord start for her, but he pulled back as Floyd grabbed an ax sticking out of the chopping block near the shed. Floyd came at him, swinging out. Cord jumped back. His foot came down on a log that rolled out from under him, dropping him to the ground. The ax cleared his head by inches.

The miss pulled Floyd off balance and he staggered, giving Cord time enough to spring to his feet and bring a branch up with him, locked firmly in his hands.

Floyd spun on him for another strike. The branch connected with the wood handle, stopping it in its descent, jarring the ax free. It landed several feet from them.

Cord tossed the branch aside, hauled back his fist and sent it solidly into the man's face, lifting him off his feet and dropping him into a heap on the ground.

Cord rushed to Eliza, reaching her just as he heard another sound behind him.

"Drop it." Cal's voice ordered, low and dangerous sounding.

Cord glanced back to see if it was directed at him. Cal had his gun out, but it was pointed directly at Huck who released a piece of wood and slowly raised his hands.

"She all right?" Cal asked.

Cord turned back to Eliza, sliding a hand behind her head.

She groaned as he touched the large bump forming, moved then groaned again. She jerked and cried out.

"It's all right. You're safe. I have you." He didn't know why he said the last, it probably wasn't very comforting but as he slid his arms around her, she leaned into him.

Her eyes were closed and he thought she might have slipped back into unconsciousness.

"Eliza." When he said her name, her eyes opened again, fluttering a bit, but not in the coy way women did when flirting.

"Oh," she gasped and pulled away, struggling to stand. Unable to do anything else, he helped her up. She whimpered and teetered.

Cord tightened his hold. Her head dropped to his shoulder and stayed. He studied the scene over her head.

Cal still had his gun drawn, pointed at the two conscious men. He directed them to the large man, who was still out cold.

Despite the throbbing in his knuckles, Cord still burned to land a few more blows.

"She all right?" Cal repeated his earlier question.

"I think so. She hit her head when that," he cut off but glared at Floyd, "Pushed her."

"Can you get her to Doc's while I take them to the jail?" the sheriff asked.

"Jail!" Huck snapped more alert and back to being belligerent. "For what?"

"Assault on a lady." Cal answered.

"We done no such thing."

"Yeah, I didn't mean to hurt her. She fell when he came barging in. We was just going to have a little fun. We'd even have paid 'er, if she wanted."

The words sent Cord's insides to boiling.

"See, we weren't doing anything wrong," Huck said, sending a glare at his companion.

"I heard." Cord said through clinched teeth.

"You heard wrong. We was just discussin' havin' a

little fun with her."

Cord felt a shiver pass through her. "She didn't want anything to do with your 'fun' or you. I heard her ask you to leave her alone."

"You misunderstood. She was just tryin' to drive up the price. Our word against yours." Huck's lips pulled up in a smile and his eyelids narrowed down. Obviously, it wasn't the first time he'd used the argument.

"Then for the night, you'll be spending it in the jail for disturbing the peace," Cal spoke up. "And, since I'm the peace officer, and it was my peace you disturbed, there's no arguing it." Cal's expression was out-right stony.

"What about him?" Huck tipped his head, sending a glare at Cord.

Cord figured the man was really stupid if he wanted to be locked in a cell with him.

Cal came up with a solution before he could express agreement with the notion. "He's just giving me a hand tonight overseeing the town. A deputy of sorts."

The two men looked like they'd argue but Cal didn't give them a chance. "Now get a hold of your friend there and carry, or drag him over to the jail. You pick. Just get him and you there. Cord." He dipped his head, and sent a grin to him. "You can get her home. I'll check on her later." The grin was replaced with a look of concern.

"I'll see to her."

Cord waited until the men were ushered away before he brought his hand up to cup her cheek. He didn't think he'd ever felt anything so soft. Not even the velvety coat of a new born foal could compare. Then she lifted her head and he couldn't think.

Fear no longer tainted her eyes. She seemed slightly confused though. She blinked a couple times and swayed. The motion pulled him back alert. "Easy. I have you."

"Mister…" She let out a little groan as she tried to think.

"Cord." He supplied his first name automatically.

"Cord." When she spoke, it was whispered right into his heart. She swallowed and steadied herself. "My head."

"You hit it hard."

She started to raise her hand, but he caught it, bringing it back to his chest.

"Don't touch it. I'll check it out." He released her hand and brought his to her head. Several long strands had come free and hung like wisps of pale moonlight around her shoulders. They caught and clung to the rough pads of his fingers. It took all his will not to dwell on how to link them together, then he touched the bump.

She flinched and choked in a cry.

"Sorry."

It was a big bump but, fortunately, it felt like the skin hadn't split. Her eyes were closed and she swayed against him.

"I'll get you to Doc's."

That had her eyes springing open. "No," she cried out. "If I go to the doctor, it'll get around town. There was enough of a spectacle this afternoon. If I bring trouble, I'll be fired. I can't afford that."

"It will be all right."

She was already shaking her head. "They are very serious when it comes to reputation."

"This wasn't your fault."

"It doesn't matter. I can't afford any smudges on my honor."

Cord didn't know what to say to that.

"It's late. I need to get back. It's almost time for lights out."

As she pulled back, she wobbled and would've fallen if he hadn't caught her. Once more, she sagged against him. Her breath came in little puffs against his neck.

He liked her height and the feel of her against him, but he wished she'd let him take her to Doc's. He understood what she was saying. It was what Cal had referred to, their word against hers as to who had started the trouble, and she would be viewed in the wrong no matter what. It gulled him.

"I'll help you to the dormitory."

She drew in a breath and raised her head. "Thank you."

Propriety had him offering her his arm, but when she still wobbled after a couple steps, he gave up on it and slid his arm around her keeping her tight to his side. They made it about half the distance when she stumbled, almost pulling away and going down.

"Enough." He lifted her into his arms.

"No," she squeaked. "You can't."

"Hush." The command surprised him as much as her.

"I'm too big to carry." It was a weak protest.

"You're tall, but so am I, so it's not a problem at all." He took several more steps before he looked down. It was a mistake.

Her face was turned up to him. Her lips were parted just inches away from his. Her mouth a tempting offering. He slowed his stride. Longing warred within him.

Slowly, she lowered her head to his shoulder, saving him from having to make the decision, especially when he was afraid he knew what it might have been. He wanted to kiss her, a woman he really didn't know and who had just been through a frightening experience and was injured. What did that say about him?

He continued on, coming to the back of the establishment. A lantern hung on the porch, illuminating two figures waiting there.

"Eliza?" A timid voice called out.

A second later one of the figures dropped from the porch and flew at them.

"What did you do to her?" The demand was full of fire, of a woman ready to do battle.

Eliza stirred in his arms but didn't raise her head.

"Shh," he said to the woman, but it seemed to have a settling effect on Eliza. "There was some trouble. She hit her head."

"Trouble?" The woman's voice was quieter but not much less sharp.

"The men from earlier today caught her walking home." He heard an intake of air from the petite woman still on the porch. She shot forward, her fear replaced with concern.

"She's all right. I heard her, and then the sheriff arrived. The men are in jail."

"I doubt that will do any good."

He recognized the bolder one now that her voice was back to normal. Hannah. "The sheriff will make sure they know they're not welcome in town any longer.

Hannah raised and lowered her head in acceptance as she laid a hand on Eliza's shoulder.

"She fell and hit her head but refused to have Doc look at it."

"I'll tend her," Hannah said.

Cord took another step forward. Both women blocked him.

"You cannot enter." The petite woman seemed to have found a little steel of her own.

"I ..." Cord realized he really couldn't enter.

"We can manager her." Hannah shook Eliza's shoulder.

This time she stirred and opened her eyes. She starred up at him confused and adorable.

"Eliza. Are you all right?" Amelia asked, stepping closer.

Slowly she turned her head, breaking eye contact with him. She blinked. "Hannah, Amelia."

"Oh, yes." The petite woman reached out and caught her hand.

Hannah laid a hand on her shoulder, giving her

support.

"I'm fine." Eliza said as if registering their worry. "I have a headache and am tired, but I was tired before."

"Can you stand?" Hannah asked.

"Yes, of course. I was a bit unsteady and C… Mr. Bartlett helped me." She glanced at him. "You can put me down now."

Cord wanted to object. Instead he crossed to the porch and set her on her feet, keeping his hand ready to catch her if needed.

She gripped the post to steady herself then her friends were there taking either side of her. He stepped back.

"Thank you, Mr. Bartlett." Eliza said, her voice soft with a slight tremor in it.

He dipped his head. "Get some rest, Miss Telford. I hope you feel better." He forced himself to walk away. At the corner of the building, he gave into the desire and looked back. The three women still stood on the porch. An unlikely trio as they couldn't be more different. Still, if he had to come up with a word for them, he guessed he'd say family, because of the fierce protectiveness he sensed they had for each other.

He was glad Eliza had friends looking out for her tonight. A pang at leaving her stirred a restless cord deep within him. Unable to do anything about it, he headed for the sheriff's office.

Cal was at his desk when he entered. He looked up. "Get Miss Eliza home?"

"She's in the hands of two of her friends. Hannah and Amelia."

He nodded. "They'll watch over her."

"What's going to happen to them?" Cord tipped his head toward the cells.

"Not as much as I wish. They'll spend the night locked up and they'll be charged a fine. Then in the morning I'll ride them out of town and stress again they're not welcome around here and better stay well away from any of the women."

Cord didn't like it but expected as much. "If you need a hand?"

Cal nodded. "The problem is, women are still a shortage around here. Men forget themselves or just don't care what's proper. Since they opened, I'm getting quite a few fools trying to sweet-talk the women away from working there. Most are just love sick and harmless. A few …"

"Where's that leave us?" Cord looked Cal right in the eyes and grinned.

Cal shrugged with a grin of his own. "I think I'll walk down there and check with Miss Hannah as to how Miss Eliza's doing."

"Miss Hannah is it. Good to know." Cord tipped his hat and left.

ଔ୬

Eliza sighed as she leaned back in her bed. It had been quite an effort just to get her up to their room. Once on the stairs, she'd gotten dizzy and went down to her knees, almost taking both Hannah and Amelia with her. Luckily, between the railing and her two friends they all made it up.

It had been much nicer in Cord Bartlett's arms. A shiver went through her she couldn't stop. She could still remember the feel of firm muscle under her cheek, and the pleasant male scent of him. It was so different and very appealing. She knew she shouldn't be thinking like that, but couldn't seem to stop.

Twice that day he had come to her rescue. Other than Matthew from Silas, and her father when she'd climbed a tree and the branch had broken and left her dangling, she'd never had anyone rescue her. She'd helped her father after her mother died, and after he remarried and Matthew came, she'd helped take care of him. When her father died, she handled everything, until Silas.

She shivered again at the thought of the man. Closing her eyes, she pushed his image from her mind. Her thoughts went right back to Cord Bartlett and his gray eyes, misty and deep. His work-roughened hands were so gentle when he touched her cheek. There seemed to be honest caring in him.

Her heart pounded, which wasn't good because it made her head pound.

"How are you feeling?" Amelia settled on the edge of the bed and touched her hand.

"Better now I'm lying down."

"Hannah will be up in a minute with some tea. She said it would help your headache. She taught me how to make it so if you need some during the night, I think I can manage." Amelia gave a smile. "It's steeping now. The sheriff stopped to check on you and is talking to her. He told me to tell you not to worry. He'll see the men leave town and that you're safe."

Amelia wrapped her fingers around hers. "I'm glad Mr. Bartlett was there." She fell silent a minute before continuing. "He makes me nervous, he's such a big man, but he was very gentle with you."

There was a perplexity in the words as if Amelia was trying to put the ideas together. Eliza just couldn't concentrate on it enough to figure it out. True, Cord Bartlett was more than a full foot taller than Amelia. He was even tall to her, but she didn't feel at all threatened by him. In fact, just the opposite, she felt comfortable, safe like she hadn't felt in a long time.

"He defended me and was very kind."

Amelia still didn't sound sure, then again Amelia didn't trust men at all. She tried hard not to flinch around them, especially when they raised their voices. From what she said, her father was a stern man with a wide cruel streak.

Eliza couldn't understand being afraid of one's own

father, but it was evident Amelia was. Hannah showed up with the tea. She looked slightly flushed when she repeated what the sheriff had said.

Eliza drank several sips, letting the warm liquid soothe her as she listened to her friends promise they would be right there if needed. Twice nightmares invaded her sleep but both times a tall, sandy-haired man with steel-gray eyes drove them away. Strong fingers grazed her cheek just before he lifted her into the safety of his arms.

"Out of bed." The sharp snap jerked her awake.

Eliza groaned as she sat up. Dizziness threatened to swamp her.

"Are you drunk? I'm telling Mrs. Hyde." Bessie flounced off before Eliza could stop her, not that she was sad to see her go. Still, it would just lead to a whole lot more trouble.

She turned her head to the window. Though the curtain was down, enough light came in around the edges for her to know the sun was well up. Eliza forced herself to stand, gripping the bedframe for a minute to steady herself before she dared step away to clean herself and dress. She was just tying her apron when the station mistress burst into the room.

"What is this that you've been drinking? You know it is not allowed. It is in the terms for being dismissed."

"I was not drinking." Eliza cut her off before the woman could get into the tirade she wasn't up to hearing right then. "I fell last night and hit my head." She glanced past the woman to where Bessie stood gloating in the doorway. "I had to take my apron to be laundered because the one who was assigned missed it though it was in the pile with the others."

"So you say." Mrs. Hyde huffed.

"It's the truth. You, yourself told me to take it off and that was when it was added to the pile. Hannah and Amelia can verify it, though you're not likely to accept their word on my account, but the sheriff can testify of the fall. He arrived right after, and being the sheriff, I would dare say his word can be accepted."

"You were alone with the man?" Bessie made it sound scandalous.

"Actually, Mr. Bartlett was there also. They both came to my assistance." Eliza couldn't help but feel a touch of glee at the expression that crossed Bessie's face. Sour didn't come near to describe it because there was too much fury in the mix that scrunched her features and colored her skin. "He was most kind and helped me back here."

Bessie's reaction to that was instantaneous. Fire blazed in her eyes, so it was surprising smoke didn't come from her nose when she huffed and turned. Her footfall thundered on the stairs.

"That may be," Mrs. Hyde broke the silence that followed after, "but you are behind on your duties and will be assigned others."

"Oh, she's not behind," Hannah spoke up from the top of the stairs. "I've taken care of all them. It was my off day, so I was able to see to it. All is done."

The supervisor looked between them. "Get to work," she snapped at Eliza and stomped out not any quieter than Bessie had.

Hannah shook her head. "Don't let her bother you."

"I don't."

"How are you this morning?"

"Better. My head's still tender," Eliza reached up and touched the spot, "and I have a slight headache, but nothing I can't handle. I'm sorry you gave up your morning."

Hannah waved the comment away. "Would you like me to take your day?"

"No, that's not necessary. I can do it. It will help me to stay busy. Thank you."

"What are friends for?"

Chapter Six

Cord stayed away from town for six days, determined not to give in to his desire to go see how Eliza was doing. Cal sent word out with his foreman that the men had grudgingly moved on. Cord hoped they'd stay gone.

He eyed the train station as he rode into town but refused to head down that way. He'd see to his business first and order the supplies he needed for the ranch, then if it was about time for lunch, he'd go. It only made sense.

Two and a half hours later he stepped through the double doors and surveyed the room. It only took a second to see Eliza wasn't there. She was a hard woman to miss, but when a minute passed and she didn't come out of the back, he started to get worried.

"Mr. Bartlett. If you're looking for a table, I have plenty room at mine right over there." The simpering quality of the voice grated on him though it was a pleasant enough voice.

He glanced at the woman and recognized her. She'd served him on his first visit and always spoke when she saw him.

"Actually, I'm joining a friend." He cut through the crowd of tables toward a dark-haired man. He'd only left Logan McKane's office at the bank an hour earlier and didn't have any need to talk with him, but he recognized the petite woman serving the table as one of Eliza's friends.

Amelia something, he didn't know her last name. Her

other friend Hannah was at the next table. One of them should be able to tell him how Eliza was, just to satisfy his curiosity.

"Mind if I join you?"

"Cord. Of course. I should have thought you'd come here to eat. Best food in town and an amazing view." The banker grinned.

Cord wondered if he should warn him of Cal's interest in Hannah then he realized his attention was focused on Amelia. That was interesting. He was just glad it wasn't Eliza. "I figured I'd grab a bite before I head back to the ranch."

Amelia stopped by the table and he gave his order, wondering how to phrase asking about Eliza. He tried to convince himself she was in the kitchen but was concerned. He decided to wait and watch for a time but by the time dessert arrived and there wasn't any sign of her, he couldn't wait.

"Excuse me, Miss Amelia." He gained the dark-haired girl's attention as she placed a piece of pie in front of him. "I don't see Miss Eliza today. She has recovered, hasn't she?"

"It's kind of you to ask. She's quite well. It's just her free day and she was going for a walk this afternoon."

"Thank you for letting me know." He wasn't sure what else to say, his thoughts already on Eliza. Where would she walk to? Was she with someone? He hadn't seen her on the streets in town. Where would he look? Not that he was interested in a walk.

He quickly took the last couple bites of pie. She really shouldn't be out alone, especially after what happened before, though it was unlikely to happen again.

"Logan." He acknowledged the man whose main focus was on the little waitress who he was still coaxing into talking to him, but she was as nervous as any filly he'd ever seen.

"Talk to you later," he said, not that the man noticed. Cord dropped some money on the table to cover the meal, picked up his hat and hurried out.

Not far away the creek that ran past his ranch cut through town. Houses butted up to it, but just outside of town was a nice little area where he knew the town's people often had picnics after church. He headed that way.

It only took him a few minutes to reach it. It really was a beautiful area with bright yellow, red, purple and blue flowers dotting the green grass. The only reason no one had claimed it was because in the heavy run off it often flooded. He glanced around. Disappointment snuck up on him until he noticed a blue patch too large to be flowers down by the bank, partially concealed by a tree trunk.

A woman sat on a downed log not far from the water. Cautiously, he moved through the grass, so not to scare her. It didn't take him long to see by the long body it was Eliza. Anticipation of seeing her hit, along with a jab of foolishness. *What had he been thinking about not needing, not wanting a woman in his life?*

He tried to convince himself to go, but before he could, she turned. A startled gasp escaped her as she spun his way, but she seemed to relax at the sight of him. He didn't know what it was about her but she was like a ray of light taken down from heaven.

"Mr. Bartlett." Her hand went to her throat, but she smiled. "You startled me."

"I apologize." He reached up to remove his hat. "How you are?"

"Fine, thank you. I guess a touch nervous." Her hands waved out before she tucked them in her lap.

He walked closer, drawn in. The blue dress brought out the blue in her eyes, even the sky couldn't compare to the color.

"This is a pretty place. Do you come here often?" she asked.

Her question surprised him. "I've come here a couple times for town socials, but no, I just don't come here. There's a place similar on my ranch." He didn't know why he told her that. No one knew that was where he liked to go for some peaceful time. "I actually was looking for you. I wanted to see how you were. You hit your head hard."

"I'm all recovered, even the bump is no longer tender." She reached up to touch the back of her head. "Or only just a bit."

"That's good." He stepped a little closer. "May I join you?" He motioned to the log.

"Please." She blushed.

He settled a couple feet from her, working his hat in his hands. "Do you like it here?"

"I love the area."

"Winter can be a little hard for a couple months, though we don't get as much snow as up north."

"I've been told that." She reached out and touched a dainty yellow wildflower.

"To me it's the right combination for cattle."

"You're a rancher?" She glanced at him.

He dipped his head in acknowledgement. "I've a place a couple miles outside of town." He waved his hat up river. "So you're going to be staying on?" He couldn't believe he asked the question.

She looked just as surprised. "I'm contracted for five more months, then I'll see."

"How'd you end up here?" He figured he'd already pressed the bounds. There was no harm going farther.

"I needed a job and a place to go. This location was available when I applied."

Her answer raised more questions. He wanted to refuse to ask but the next slipped out. "You didn't want to stay at home?"

She glanced away. "It's … it's not that easy."

Cord didn't think she was going to say more, but she

fixed her gaze on the other side of the stream and started to talk. "My mother died when I was young. My father remarried. My stepmother is a nice, gentle souled woman, but." Eliza swallowed, the emotion building in her. "My father died a year ago. He left us well taken care of, but my stepmother remarried a couple months back. I couldn't stay." The last words poured out of her with threads of stress.

He knew there was more she wasn't quite telling him, but he'd finally caught his tongue and didn't pry deeper.

"I'm surprise you didn't marry and stay close to home."

She jerked as if he'd slapped her. "I ... I ought to leave." She stood.

"Please don't go." He caught her hand. The awareness that had been floating in the air ignited.

She gasped as she looked back. Out from under the tree the sun fell on her, setting her to glow. Her eyes were wide and perfectly matched the color of the sky.

"I apologize. I had no right to pry." He ran his thumb over the smooth skin, taken by how soft it was.

"I ... I."

"I'm sorry. What would you like to talk about?"

She relaxed and with a slight tug, she settled back down on the log, just on the opposite side of him from where she'd originally been sitting. "Tell me about your ranch?"

He released her hand, immediately missing the feel of it. "It's a ranch. What's to tell?" He wanted to tell her about every inch of it, the cattle and the house, but didn't truly think she cared.

"I've never seen much of a real ranch before."

That took him by surprise. "My ranch is pretty fair sized. I have twenty-seven horses, and a hundred and eighty head of cattle."

"One hundred and eighty?" Astonishment widened her

eyes.

"I've been busy building up my herd. I still plan to add a few more cows, but I have it pretty much how I want it."

"How do you feed that many?"

"I have a lot of real good land. I also have a few good hands that help me."

"It still seems like so many."

"It's a fair number. Why don't we take a ride out there sometime so I can show you?" He was surprised at his invitation and even more when she smiled at him with longing in her eyes, then she looked down. "You've never been on a horse?" he ventured a guess.

She raised her gaze. "Not since I was little. I actually had my own pony, but that was a long time ago and nothing like you see around here. I used to ride with my father." A fond look crossed her face.

"Sounds like you need a lesson. We still have plenty of time today."

"Today?" She brightened.

"My horse is just at the edge of town, not far from here. We can get him if you'd like to try?" He wanted her to accept the invitation more than anything.

"You don't have to get back to your ranch?"

"Not right now."

Her lip caught between her teeth as she hesitated. "I would really like to try. If you're certain you have the time and don't mind."

"I'm sure." He stood, and didn't have to wait for her to follow.

Then she looked down at her dress. "Can I ride in this?"

He pushed back his hat and arched a brow. He hadn't thought about it. "Well, a side saddle might be easier, but my saddle would be steadier. Most women around here just use the regular saddle. It'll be trickier getting on, but once settled your skirt should be full enough to be modest for you. If you're okay with that?"

She nodded.

He offered her his arm and she laid her hand on it. The touch of her fingers on his wrist heightened the sense of awareness that had been humming through him. He drew in a breath and picked up a soft floral scent that wasn't from any of the flowers in the meadow. Everything about her was intriguing and beautiful.

It didn't take long to reach where he had his horse tethered. He was glad he'd chosen to ride Rufus there that day instead of one of the ones he was still working on gentling. The gelding was one of the best-tempered horses he owned.

"This here's Rufus. He's a good natured horse. Sure footed and steady as they come." He wondered if she'd be a little nervous, but she went right up to the large animal without hesitation and let him smell her hand.

She smiled at the touch of his nose. "He reminds me of my father's horse, but he had a white blaze."

"You seem to like horses," he observed.

She nodded.

"But you don't ride?"

"My stepmother is deathly afraid of them. Her first husband was killed in a riding accident. She sold my father's horse after he died, so all we have is a couple of carriage horses. Mostly, we walked places."

"As I said, Rufus here is a real nice horse." He scratched behind the horse's ears. "He'll be on his best behavior." He looked around the area. "Why don't we go back to the meadow? It's more private."

"All right."

Again she moved easily beside him.

ଓଞ୍ଚ

Eliza couldn't believe what she was doing. First, she'd sat and talked with Cord Bartlett, totally unchaperoned, which would have shocked her stepmother, but she hadn't felt nervous about it at all.

At least not worried nervous. She couldn't quite identify what hummed through her. Excitement was part of it and if being honest, not all due to the prospect of riding a horse. Eliza had to admit she found him attractive. What surprised her was he was so easy to talk with, and he listened.

She liked the way he talked and looked at her. She'd say there was interest in his eyes, but not the kind that said he wanted to possess her, like a valuable object to be displayed. She knew that look all too well, the adoring, put her on a pedestal and then talk to her like she didn't have a brain or wasn't truly real. Just a pampered piece of porcelain.

Cord was going to let her ride his horse. Teach her to ride. Since she arrived out west and seen everyone on horses, she'd wanted to ride desperately. She'd really loved her pony when she was little, especially its bumpy trot that used to rattle her insides and make them feel all funny, not unlike how this man made her feel.

"Are you nervous?"

His question took her by surprise. Eliza hadn't realized she'd grown so quiet. "Not at all. I've been wanting to ride."

"I can't image a day not being on a horse. I don't think I would do well living in the city."

"It's nothing like being here."

He frowned slightly so she tried to explain. "Here it's open with a sky you can see forever and the sunsets, I've never seen anything so beautiful. I like to be in the dining room at that time of day. The light comes in through the big windows and the room is awash in light."

"My house on the ranch has windows that face the mountains so the morning light flows in but the evening light shines back off the mountains and glows through the room. It's a good way to end the day." He glanced over at her, looking a touch sheepish. "Ready to get on."

She nodded not daring to try voicing the words.

He turned and patted the horse's neck. "Why don't you step up here?" He directed her to the downed tree they'd sat and talked on. "Then you can step over. It should be easier to position your skirt. I think it's full enough to be decent. Other women do it around here. Though if you do a lot of riding, you might want to get a riding outfit that is split. I've seen a few of those."

She'd seen them too, just doubted she could afford one anytime soon. "All right." She stepped to the log trying to figure out how she was going to get on it any easier than the horse. Before she could come up with a plan, Cord's large hands closed around her waist. She gasped as he lifted her easily off the ground and set her on the log, then held her steady until she got her balance.

Eliza turned part way, resting her hand on his shoulder. He caught her other hand and she got lost looking down into his up-turned face.

For a moment, she forgot how to breathe as she gazed into cloud filled eyes. Eliza could swear lightning crackled from them. She tingled all over from the electrical storm.

"Ready?" His voice rumbled like thunder into her heart.

It was the snort of the horse that brought her back to reality. "Yes." She swallowed. "What should I do?"

"Just hold my hand. Step over. Watch your skirt and ease down onto his back. Don't worry, I'll catch you if you fall."

Eliza wondered if she hadn't already fallen, but of a totally different kind. Still she did as instructed. Rufus shifted just as she plopped on his back, but once more one of Cord's hands spanned her waist, steadying her as he held the reins firm in his other hand.

"Easy," he said softly, which immediately settled her and the horse.

Eliza took a breath. She was on a horse. She wanted to shout with pleasure, instead just beamed down at the man that made it happen.

Cord smiled up at her. "You like it."

"Yes!"

"Well, I better shorten these stirrups so you can ride. You have long legs but mine are still longer."

Eliza was aware of his hands bumping her ankles, then he fitted her foot into the stirrup before going to the other side and repeating the process.

"That should be better." The rumble in his voice sounded stronger, but he stepped back and patted the horse's neck. "Take him for a circle."

She didn't need any further encouragement. She nudge the horse softly in the side just like she used to do with her pony. Rufus started off, following her directions. They made one loop then a second before she nudged Rufus again. The horse picked up speed, moving into a trot that had her bouncing wildly in the saddle.

Cord laughed as she approached. "Take it more with your legs. He has a rough trot but his gallop is as smooth as butter. Just like sitting in a rocking chair."

She drew the horse to a stop beside him. She didn't think when he lifted his hands to her, but leaned over, placing her hands on his shoulders as his closed around her waist. She met his gaze as he lifted her off, lowering her to the ground in front of him.

Once more Eliza found herself slipping into the misty depths. Her heart quickened. Her body heated like she was standing too close to a roaring fire, but she trembled.

Cord's head dipped. Rufus nickered and bumped his arm.

Eliza stumbled back, feeling the heat she experienced burn her cheeks.

"I better be getting back. It's getting late." Eliza clasped her hands in front of her.

"I'll walk you." He caught the horse's reins, this time not offering her his arm.

Eliza fell into step with him. Was he actually going to kiss her? Would she have let him if he tried?

She was afraid the answer was a resounding yes. She glanced over at him, homing in on his intriguing mouth. His lips were firm, jaw set. He didn't look her way, and she wondered if it all had been her imagination.

At the moment, he seemed more like a granite statue than the man who had smiled at her as she rode around the meadow. Pleasure hummed again at the thought. She'd ridden a horse. She wanted to go again. Maybe on her next free day. She wished she could ask Cord, but knew that was unacceptable.

"Thank you for letting me ride your horse," she said politely, trying to rein in her exuberance to what would be proper. "I enjoyed it very much."

"You're welcome." He finally looked her way, but didn't linger. "You did very well."

"It wasn't any different from when I was younger on my pony but maybe more exciting."

He glanced again, longer this time and his firm lips twitched slightly at one corner. "I'd say you liked it."

Her excitement surged forward before she could pull it back. "Oh, yes. I can't wait to do it again." She bit her lip to gain control. "I wonder how much the livery charges to ride?"

He frowned. "Don't worry about it. When you can go, I'll make arrangements. I'd sooner see you on a horse I know," he added quickly.

Eliza cleared the corner of the building as a thrill surged through her.

"And just what do you think you're doing?" Mrs. Hyde's verbal slap made Eliza jerk. Fury burned off the woman who stood waiting on the porch with her hands on her hips, like she'd been waiting a long time.

Eliza froze. "It is my free day."

"And you think that means I wouldn't know you sent a letter to the head office?"

"I ..."

Cord stepped around the corner as the woman burst out, cutting her off. "You think I wouldn't find out."

"I don't know what you're talking about."

Mrs. Hyde glanced from her to Cord. "Who is Matthew Brown?"

"My brother."

"Your name is Telford," she snapped, as if annoyed at having to remind her.

"He's my half-brother," Eliza said as if that actually explained it.

Her supervisor studied her a moment, her lips in a way that crinkled her face in an unattractive sneer. "We'll talk about this later." With that she turned and went inside.

"Is there a problem?"

Eliza jerked. The confrontation with Mrs. Hyde had momentarily wiped Cord from her mind.

"I don't think so. I'm not sure why she would be upset at me for sending a letter. Or how she'd even know where it's going and to who." She thought of Mrs. Hyde using her brother's name, actually it was the last name of their next door neighbor who she was sending the letters to for her brother.

"It's not that big of a town that people don't know each other and everybody's business."

She nodded, wondering what new trouble was brewing. Eliza pushed the gloomy thought away and turned back to the man beside her. "Thank you for the ride and the afternoon."

"It was my pleasure. Your next free day I'll take you to the ranch. If you'd like?"

"I would like that." Right now, she wanted it more than anything. "It's not for another two weeks." Would he retract his invitation? She glanced up, trying to read his thoughts. It was still odd having to look up at a man. Her heart fluttered at the intensity in his gaze.

"I'll keep it in mind and be in touch." His words were slow and casual. He tipped the brim of his hat and walked off.

Eliza stared after him, trying to calm her insides. She really didn't know much about him, but more than she did any other men, including all those that asked for her hand. He was going to take her riding out to his ranch. Was that an acceptable thing out west?

Another delightful tingle raced through her. She really didn't care. She wanted to go riding again. She wanted to see the ranch he so obviously loved. In truth, she wanted to spend more time with Cord Bartlett.

That wasn't proper. Her insides fluttered and she pushed it away. Not that her thoughts truly left him.

She concentrated on his ranch, wondering what it was really like. Just the spark in his eyes said he was proud of what he'd built. She'd seen a couple ranches that were close to town when she went walking with Hannah and Amelia. One was big and fancy. A couple were small with rough houses. Most were in between those extremes.

She didn't see Cord settling for small and rough. Everything about him suggested to her a drive to work hard for what he wanted. Still this was a young growing area.

Her thoughts were still on Cord as she stepped through the door and into a rolling pin. Only the instinctual flinch at the blurred motion saved her from taking the blow on the side of her head. With a rush of air it swished by her head, glancing off her shoulder in its downward arch.

Chapter Seven

Eliza cried out and dropped to the floor as much from shock as pain.

"I told you to stay away from him." Malice spewed from Bessie as she stormed off.

Eliza sat, stupefied at the woman's violent attack. The gravy was one thing but this. She moved her arm. The muscle was sore but eased. She was fortunate it didn't hit her head and knock her out, or hit the top of her shoulder and break a bone. As it was, she'd have a bruise and it would be tender for a couple days.

The debate was whether to report the attack. Eliza had her doubts that much would be done but decided she couldn't just let it stand.

Pulling herself off the floor, she stopped to rub the muscle before going to find Mrs. Hyde. The woman was actually in the overseer's office, just off the worker's entrance by the kitchen.

Eliza stood in the doorway a full minute before the woman deemed to look at her. "Yes," she said curtly.

"I want to lodge a complaint against one of the women." Eliza stepped into the room.

"Did anyone else see this attack?"

Eliza caught her word usage. So Mrs. Hyde already knew and was as much saying she wouldn't do anything about it. Still Eliza pressed on.

"No, there was no one else in the room."

"Then it will be your word against hers. I'm afraid I can't accept that. Your petty differences have no place in the work here."

"Petty difference. She hit me with a rolling pin and you know it."

"I know no such thing," the supervisor snapped. "Except ..." she drew the word out, "that you are a problem causer, believing you should get preferential treatment. Well, that will not happen."

"When have I asked for preferential treatment?"

The woman didn't deem to answer. "You are receiving a warning. Two more mishaps and you will be let go."

"I'm receiving." Eliza bit back saying anything else and turned away, knowing she'd just get blamed for more.

"You may be dismissed." The words followed her.

Eliza went out the backdoor, fuming. She longed to let the woman know exactly what she thought, but she needed this job. Eliza paced, trying to get herself back under control. She knew she should go in and eat but just couldn't manage it just then.

Her shoulders slumped. It had been such a beautiful day. One of the best she'd ever had. Her mind slipped back over the details, the exultant feel of riding, flutters that tickled her senses when she looked into Cord's misty gray eyes. She wrapped her arms around her waist as she did the memories around her heart.

No matter what Bessie threatened or did, if Cord Bartlett invited her to go riding again, she would accept the offer. She'd just have to be a little more careful and watch out for the woman.

A shiver of excitement went through her as his image filled her mind.

He was such a handsome man. One of the most handsome she'd ever seen, but she knew better than anyone that appearance was only skin deep. Men had forever been drawn to her because of her looks, wanted her because she was beautiful, but never even tried to get to know her. She could've been awful, like Bessie and they wouldn't have noticed.

She didn't want to be foolish like that. She wanted a man she could respect and love. Not that she was out to find love, she reaffirmed sternly to herself, but the image of Cord on his horse came back to her mind. He was an amazing figure, but she liked the spark in his eyes when he talked about his ranch. That fit him.

He'd also been truly magnificent when he'd come to her rescue, though it was slightly blurry in her mind. One thing she did remember was how tender he'd been with her. He'd made her feel safe, cared for.

Had he really been going to kiss her? Heat flushed her cheeks. For a moment she let herself dream.

Finally the noisy clatter of pots and pans being washed permeated her reverie. The night cleanup had begun. If she wanted anything to eat, she better hurry.

She was relieved to find Amelia and Hannah just sitting down with their food when she entered. She wouldn't have to eat alone. Quickly, she filled a plate and joined them.

"Hi," Amelia greeted. "How was your day?"

"Wonderful." She tried to hold back the excitement that wanted to burst out. "I got to ride a horse."

"Really." Amelia's eyes grew bright. She was becoming more expressive every day. "How did you manage that?" She made it sound like a great feat.

"I ran into Mr. Bartlett. He let me ride his horse in the meadow by the stream."

Hannah arched her brow but didn't say anything, letting her expectant look say it all, like she was so good at.

Eliza felt her face heat. "What?" She broke the silence.

"He just let you ride his horse?" Hannah asked directly.

"Yes. We were talking and I mentioned I hadn't been

on a horse since I was a child and that was actually a pony."

"I've never been on a horse." Amelia said softly. "My father—" She broke off, not saying anymore.

Eliza got the reference and could've finished the sentence. Her father wouldn't have approved of her being on a horse. He certainly wouldn't have approved of Amelia talking to a man. Amelia hadn't been allowed to do anything but sit and be a show piece.

"It was a lot of fun." Eliza let her pleasure show to ease the tension. "I didn't try to run the horse but the trot was so bouncy it rattled my teeth."

"I don't know if that sounds fun." Hannah said.

Eliza already knew she hadn't ever ridden a horse either. "It was." She was grinning and couldn't stop.

"Just don't let Bessie see you with him. He's one of the ones she has her eye on." Amelia cautioned.

Eliza's smile slipped. "She already did."

"What happened?" Hannah leaned forward over the table.

Eliza explained the details of the attack.

"Did you report her?" Amelia asked.

"Yes."

"But..." Hannah started then stopped, looking concerned.

"I received a warning." Eliza got out through her frustration.

"What?" Amelia burst.

Eliza nodded. "I'm not to let it affect my work. Two more warnings and I'll be fired."

"That's just wrong." Amelia crossed her arms in front of her and blew out a breath.

"Yes, but Mrs. Hyde makes the rules," Hannah acknowledged the problem. "What are you going to do?"

"Try not to get anymore warnings." Eliza shrugged with the futility of the situation.

Cঙৌৎ

For two weeks everything went smoothly. Even Bessie pretty much avoided her due to the fact Hannah made sure all the other girls heard what Bessie had done. So all but Bessie's three underlings avoided Bessie like the plague. Eliza didn't think Bessie minded much as long as she still had her little group to boss around and tell her how marvelous she was.

Eliza also managed to stay in Mrs. Hyde's good graces, which wasn't easy because the supervisor was always looking for any slight.

It might have helped that she only saw Cord twice in that time period. Once he'd passed her on the street and tipped his hat at her, the other time he'd come in for a meal and managed to sit at one of her tables. He asked when she'd be free to go riding, which at the time was nearly a week away.

Mrs. Hyde had been watching, curtailing any real conversation, but just seeing him had lifted her spirits. Now it was just a couple more hours and it would be her free day. She hoped Cord really would remember.

Eliza placed the plate on the table and hurried to the next. The Westerly train would be pulling out in just thirty-four minutes and everyone was clamoring for a good meal before the evening train got on its way. She took the orders and was back at the table in under two minutes with their food. That was how the next twenty-seven minutes went by in a blur of activity giving her nary a chance to get in a breath.

When the boarding call came in and the people filed out, it brought a sigh of relief as she looked over the nearly empty room. Usually the view out the large windows captured her gaze but this evening a lone figure snagged and held it.

Unable to believe her eyes, she'd took four steps forward before his name slipped out. "Matthew." She rushed across the room meeting him halfway as he dove into her arms. She pulled him to her.

He'd grown, she thought as she hugged him tight. He was really there.

"Matthew," she pushed him back. "What are you doing here?" She noticed a yellowish, green discoloration around one eye. "Silas!" Shock seized her muscles, freezing her. "He hit you!" Fury freed her. "Are you all right?" She tipped his head from side to side, hunting for other marks.

"I'm all right, 'Liza," he said bravely but there was a tremor in his voice.

"Where's your mother?"

"She's at home. I couldn't stay."

"What's going on here?" Mrs. Hyde's waspish voice picked up tempo. "Who is this?"

Eliza turned to beseech the woman for some leniency so she could deal with her brother but didn't see much that gave her hope. "This is my brother, Matthew. He's come a long way. May I take a minute to get him settled then I'll finish my work for the day?"

The woman scowled. Eliza was about to give up when Mrs. Hyde gave a small nod.

"Thank you."

The woman huffed. "One minute." Her nose high she walked off.

"Have you had anything to eat?" Eliza turned to her brother.

Matthew shook his head. "Not since this morning. It took longer than I thought to get here."

"All right. Sit here and I'll get you something." She directed him to one of her tables and went to get him some food. When she returned, Amelia stood next to him.

"I don't have any brothers or sisters for that matter. There was always just me. You are very fortunate." She was saying.

"I am." Eliza said placing the plate in front of him.

"Eat up while I finish cleaning off the other tables. I'll get you some dessert when you're done."

Matthew dug into the food like a starving hound dog, which wasn't odd for him, but concerned her. Eliza wished she could stay with him and talk but didn't dare. Still she kept an eye on him as she moved around the room.

It was impossible to ignore the bruise on his cheek. She couldn't believe Silas had hurt him. Silas was always careful around Matthew, afraid of raising his mother's wrath. Eliza wondered what else had changed since she'd left. What else had Silas done that made Matthew run to her?

She shuddered and doubled her effort in getting her work done so they could talk. She was also going to have to find a place for him to stay, because it was certain he wouldn't be allowed to stay with her.

She glanced at her brother and this time noticed Hannah had stopped to talk to him before turning to her tables.

Eliza had just finished stacking clean plates and linens to set out when Mrs. Hyde appeared. "There are more waiting in the kitchen. Remember you need to set tonight, and don't be thinking of passing it off on your friends to do."

"I'll make sure it is all set and ready for the morning," Eliza assured.

"You need to think of something to do with your brother. Where's your parents?"

For the first time Eliza thought she heard a hint of compassion in the woman's voice. "Our father is dead. His mother is home. I don't know any more yet."

"You'll have to find him a place to stay. It's against the rules for him to stay upstairs."

Eliza nodded. She knew the rules but wanted to argue them. He was still a boy. A boy that had come half way across the country on his own. Eliza blinked back tears that threatened, catching another glimpse of him before going to the next tray of dishes and silver.

When she came back in, Hannah was seated next to the sheriff at the table with her brother. It looked like Hannah made introductions before standing and heading toward her.

"Well, that's settled," Hannah said as she approached.

"What is?" Eliza couldn't fathom what she was talking about.

"Where Matthew will stay. He can't stay here. You know it won't be allowed."

Eliza was already nodding her affirmation.

"You can't stay in one of the rooms in town and wouldn't want him staying on his own. Who could be safer and more trustworthy than Sheriff Cal Steadman?"

"I doubt the sheriff will want to watch after a boy."

"You'll be watching him, the sheriff just agreed he could stay with him while Matthew was here or you could make other arrangements. Don't worry, the sheriff will keep an eye on him."

"He agreed? You already asked him?"

"Yes. He said he'd pick him up on his last foray through town."

"I can't believe you asked him, and he accepted."

Hannah shrugged but her cheeks pinked a little. "Yes, well. The sheriff has that big house he's fixing up. And he's a good man."

"And he's sweet on you." Eliza leaned in and whispered.

The color deepened on Hannah's cheeks to no missing the blush. Her friend looked away. "More like every other male. It's you he wants."

Eliza shook her head, knowing better. Hannah might not be ready to accept the truth yet, but the sheriff only had eyes for her friend since he saw Hannah. "Thank you."

Hannah hurried away as Eliza headed for the table.

"Good evening, Sheriff."

"Miss Eliza." He rose slightly and bowed his head.

"What can I get for you tonight?"

"I think I'll have what your brother is having. Matthew says it's good."

"I'll be right back." She hurried away, taking stock of everyone remaining in the restaurant. Fortunately it was a light evening. If no one else came in they'd be closing in less than a half hour. She prayed no one else came in.

Serving up a large portion of Roast beef, potatoes and carrots, she picked up the plate and a small basket of golden-brown rolls, and turned in time to see Cord Bartlett come through the door. Her breath caught as his path brought him to her just as she placed the sheriff's meal in front of him.

Cord settled at the table. "Eliza, how are you this evening?" he greeted.

"Fine, thank you." In truth she wasn't sure how she was but confused and her heart just took another jump in seeing him.

"That looks good. I'll have the same." He place his hat on the chair next to him and brushed back his hair. "Who do we have here?"

Eliza heard the question as she left the table.

"This is Matthew, Miss Eliza's brother. It seems he's come to pay her a visit." Eliza heard Sheriff Steadman answer and had to fight the urge to glance back to see if she could gage Cord's reaction. She didn't know why it mattered to her.

೮೩೮೦

Cord watched Eliza walk away then turned back to her brother. There a resemblance in the chin and cheek bones but where Eliza was fair-haired and blue-eyed, Matthew's hair was darker and he had dark, soulful brown eyes.

A fading yellow and blueish-green were evident

around his left eye. Cord's pulse quicken and this time it wasn't from being around Eliza. Someone had hit the boy. Automatically, his hand tightened into a fist. With force of will he uncurled his fingers placing his hand flat on the table.

"When did you arrive Matthew?"

"On the late train," the boy said after swallowing his food.

"That must have been some ride. You make it all by yourself?"

Matthew nodded. Looking toward Eliza with his fork halfway to his mouth, he shifted in his seat and glanced at Cal.

"You're the sheriff. That means you protect people?" the boy asked seriously.

Cord exchanged looks with Cal and leaned forward.

"Someone out to hurt you?" Cal asked.

Matthew shifted his gaze to Eliza and back, then shook his head.

"Does someone want to hurt Eliza?" Cord didn't like the thought but had to ask and wasn't surprised at the answer.

"Silas found out where she is. I didn't tell. Honest. Even after he hit me."

Cord's chest tightened, making it impossible to get anything out. Fortunately Cal asked the question trapped inside.

"Who's Silas?"

"He's our stepfather. But he's not a good man, not like our father was. And he wants to hurt Eliza.

Cord looked up to see Eliza standing several feet away. The tray trembled in her hands. Before Cord could stand, Hannah stepped up and took it from her.

"Here," she said then set the plate in front of him.

"Miss Eliza, will you sit down please?" Cal motioned to the table.

"Eliza, sit. You need to talk with them." Hannah urged her to the table. "I'll be back with dessert and a nice calming cup of tea for you." She directed the last to Eliza.

Eliza sank into a chair. In a sudden action, she pulled Matthew into her arms hugging him tight. "I'm sorry. I never thought he'd hurt you to find me."

The boy squirmed a little but didn't try to pull away for some time. When he did, he swallowed hard. "He hit me because I sassed him. Silas was huffing around the house. He's more furious every day. Mama is mad at him. She yelled at him for running you off. She won't even talk to him."

A sheen of moisture filled Matthew's eyes. "He says he knows where you are and going to get you. He said you were sinful to be running off from your family and that he'd have to watch you and teach you better or no man would be safe from wanting you."

Cord could hardly believe what he was hearing. Eliza had her hand up, covering her mouth, but he could still see the quivering in her lips. The fear in her eyes tore at him. He wanted to wipe it away.

Cord followed her panicked gaze as it dart around the room. To his relief, the room was empty but for the four women cleaning up and two of them he recognized as her friends. The doors had been closed for the evening.

"Where are you going to go?" Matthew's voice rose with his fear, causing it to crack.

"I ... I." She tried to get out words but her voice failed her.

The thought of her leaving and alone in the world petrified him. "She not going anywhere." The words came from him before Cord realized he was the one saying them.

"He's right." Cal took over. "Could be it's just a ploy to frighten you." Cal exchanged looks with him. "But even if he does know, here you have friends that will help look out after you."

When he paused Cord started again, looking right at her. "When you are at work you have people around you. Other times, stay close to Hannah, Amelia and the other ladies. There is safety in the group. Is it permitted that Matthew can stay here?"

Eliza shook her head, worrying her bottom lip with her teeth.

"Okay. I'll take him out to the ranch with me. Your free day is still day after tomorrow?" Cord asked what he'd originally come to town to find out.

She nodded.

"Then in the morning, I'll come get you and you can spend the day there with him."

"And I can keep an eye out for anyone asking about you," Cal spoke up. "I'm sure Hannah, Amelia and several of the other ladies will help look out for anyone interested in you."

Matthew, who had sat silent, now spoke up. "You'll protect her? Silas is mean. I think he is crazy."

"We'll protect her. Out here we watch out for each other," Cal said.

"And, we protect our women," Cord added. "No one will harm Eliza while I have a breath in my body." The vow came strong from his heart as he met her gaze.

Her eyes went wide and mouth opened in a sweet little O. Gradually, it shifted into a weak smile. "Thank you." The words were whispered as trust slipped passed fear.

He dipped his head.

"We're settled then. I'll talk to Hannah, Amelia, and Mrs. Hyde, and I'll let them pass the information along. Tell me exactly what your stepfather looks like."

"He's about my height. A big man, somewhat portly, but not tall. His face is pudgy, with jowls. His nose is wide, kind of flat." Eliza shuddered. "His eyes are so dark they don't even look brown. His brows are bushy, and salt and pepper like his hair with more white that black."

"Mama wishes she wouldn't have married him. She thought that we needed a father, but he isn't a good man," Matthew said, his voice firmer now.

Cord guessed he was repeating what he'd overheard, but figured he'd have to agree. He could understand wanting Eliza, but the way it sounded was just plain wrong.

"We'll have to let your mother know you're here safe." Eliza placed her hand over her brother's and squeezed. "She'll be worried sick."

"But if you send a telegram he might see it." Matthew pointed out what came immediately to Cord's mind.

Eliza again worried her bottom lip.

He would always know when she was troubled. "I can send it. Your stepfather wouldn't know me, but is there a way to make sure just your mother saw it?"

"Mrs. Brown." Matthew answered first. "She lives next-door. She's who Eliza sent her letters to me through. She knows what's wrong. She's who helped me buy my ticket for the train and gave me food. She won't tell. She thinks Mr. Marsh is a hypocrite among other things. Going to church on Sunday and thinking those thoughts."

Cord found his lip wanting to twitch. He liked the boy. "So if I send a message to her, she'd get it to your mother?"

"Yes." Eliza took over. "She'd be willing to help."

"All right. We missed the telegraph tonight but I can come back to town and send it in the morning."

"Why don't I send the message so you don't have to make the trip?" Cal offered.

Cord nodded his agreement though he wanted to come check on her for his own peace of mind. "Then I'll be here in the morning of the next day to get her, but if there's trouble, you'll let me know?"

With the agreement from Cal, Cord focused on Eliza. "You can visit a while before we head to the ranch." He picked up his hat, not wanting to leave her, but willing to give her room for some private time with her brother.

"I'll go talk to Miss Amelia and Hannah." Cal excused himself.

CRBO

Eliza looked around and realized her friends were just finishing setting the tables. She hadn't even noticed when they came and cleared their dishes. It looked like the evening work was all completed except for their table.

Eliza wasn't sure what to say. She never expected any of this. She knew Hannah and Amelia would try to help her, but to have these two men, one she'd barely met in passing, the other – she wasn't sure what to think about Cord Bartlett.

For the sheriff she could see it might be part of his job, but for Cord, coming to her aid seemed just as natural to him. Then there was her last free day. It had been one of the best days of her life. As she'd done over the last two weeks, she wondered if he really had been going to kiss her.

She ripped her mind away from the possibility and back to the problem at hand. Was she really in danger? Would Silas really come after her, or was it his blustering banter.

One look at the fading color on Matthew's face, and she was afraid she knew the answer. Uneasiness bumped up. She pushed it aside. "Matthew, would you like to go for a walk and see the town?"

"Yes." His youthful exuberance came back in his voice. "It was a long train ride." He stood, slid his chair in and reached for her hand. "There was a family with two girls. One was close to my age. I slept by them last night, and she gave me breakfast this morning. They got off two stops back."

Cord led them out onto the board walk.

"It's pretty here, but I thought there'd be more mountains," Matthew commented.

"Up north of here there is." Cord spoke up over their

shoulders.

Eliza realized he'd followed them out and was keeping an eye on them.

"We set just on the edge of the range. A nice little valley with good land and water. We've got a real pretty lake not far from here. I'll take you out to it when Eliza comes out to visit."

"Can we get to it in a buggy?" Matthew asked glancing at her.

"Sure," Cord said. "But Eliza likes to ride, so we'll go by horseback."

"You can ride, Liza?" Matthew looked shocked.

"It had been a long time since I was young, but Mr. Bartlett let me ride his horse the other day."

"Can I ride a horse? Please?"

"Sure."

There was a warm chuckle in the man's short answer that filled her with pleasure.

"That's how we get around out here. You'll have to ride with me to the ranch. I have a horse there I can bet you will like, and I have a mare with a mane about the same color as your sister's hair, that I think she'd look right fine on."

"Hear that, Eliza?"

"I hear."

"Don't worry. I'll have him riding like a cowboy by the time you get there," Cord said as if to relieve her worry, but she hadn't even been concerned. Instinctively, she knew Cord would look after her brother and he'd be a good teacher.

"I don't know how to thank you."

"You just did. Besides, as I said earlier, out here we take care of our own."

Take care of our own. Warmth rushed through her. Eliza looked around at the town then up at the man who'd moved to stand beside her. Her heart pounded with the idea that she could belong here, belong to him. It was foolish, still it gave her a thrill.

"Now, why don't you visit with your brother, and I'll just drift back a little and give you some privacy. I'll be close if you need me."

Eliza had a hard time removing her attention from the man as he stepped back.

"Eliza, I like it here." Matthew's voice called her back to him.

She looked down at her little brother. "I like it, too." She truly did, and she'd hate to leave here if Silas did come after her.

"The people here," Matthew broke off but he didn't have to say more.

She hugged him to her and glanced at the man standing guard behind them. "Now, tell me everything else that has happened."

Chapter Eight

Cord stayed about ten feet back giving them privacy but security. In all honesty, it was as far away as he could bring himself to get from her. He'd been drawn to her before but now, knowing she could possibly be in danger tore at him. He would've helped any woman in need but this woman – what would she say if he told her he felt she was his to protect?

He shook his head at the lunacy of the notion. Just a month ago, at first seeing her, he'd worked to convince himself he didn't need a woman in his life. Now he was thinking this one was his.

The image of her riding across the meadow, sunlight beaming down on her, hardly compared to the radiance of her smile when she'd looked at him as he lifted her down into his arms, down into his heart.

Cord tried not to pay attention to the conversation going on in front of him, but a portion of it drifted back.

Matthew's voice was excited as he told her about the train ride. It grew quiet and somber talking about his mother and picked up anger at his stepfather. Cord felt the boy's helplessness. He knew the feeling well. He'd lost his own father as a small boy. His mother had struggled to provide for him, his brother and sister. Then in one swoop, illness took his sister and then his mother who just didn't have the strength to go on any longer.

He hadn't been much older than Matthew at the time,

his brother, Heath, who was just two years older, when they lost their family. They'd survived together for about three years before he'd decided to make a break and go out on his own. The farm was Heath's and he was welcome to it.

Cord had never really seen himself as a farmer and he'd never regretted his decision to leave. It hadn't always been easy. In fact, it was a lot of hard work, but he'd do it all again.

He'd hired out to ranches and learned it was what he wanted. It wasn't long before he'd worked his way up to being a foreman and started building his own herd. Fortune had led him here and when the opportunity came, he got his own ranch. The hard work hadn't ended then, but it had paid off. He was where he wanted to be today.

It didn't take them long to make their circuit around town and end up back at the restaurant. Hannah and Amelia waited on the porch with Cal.

"Everything will be just fine," Hannah said as they approached. "We can keep an eye on her."

Cord wasn't sure who Hannah was talking to, him or Matthew, not that it mattered.

Hannah placed her hands on her hips and straightened. "She won't go anywhere alone."

"We gathered a couple treats for you for the ride." Amelia was more hesitant in speaking out. "I didn't know how far it was."

"Not too far, just a good stretch."

"Why don't you borrow my spare horse?" Cal suggested. "You can bring her back when you come for Miss Eliza. I have a saddle for her you can use too. She's older but dependable."

"That'd be appreciated." Cord dipped his head in acknowledgement.

"I'll get her."

"I'll get Rufus and meet you back here if you ladies won't mind waiting just a bit?"

"We'll be fine."

"So you're going out to Mr. Bartlett's ranch to stay?" Hannah drew Matthew into a conversation as he and Cal left to get the horses.

"So what do you think? Is there cause for concern?" Cord asked when they were out of hearing range, hoping Cal would say no.

"I've seen men do a lot of things I never would have believed for hate, anger and greed. I'm afraid I can't see lust as any different."

"Hearing her and Matthew talk, I'm afraid you're right. I'd say she got out of there just in time, but he might not let it end. A couple things Matthew said makes this man sound plain crazy. You might want to talk to Logan about giving you a hand if you need help."

"Logan? Why him?"

"Because if Miss Amelia asked or if he thought she could be in jeopardy, I'm sure he'd put all his resources at your use."

"Miss Amelia, huh?" Cal arched his brow.

"That's what it appeared to me the other day."

"He'll have a right fine time catching her. She's a skittish little filly."

Cord had to laugh after thinking the same thing himself. "See you back there."

They spilt directions. Cord's thoughts were not far from Eliza.

Everything was much the same as it had been when he left. Matthew leaned into Eliza, and she had her arm around him. The bond was so plain to see it could have almost been mother to son.

He'd had that close link to his mother and wondered what it would have been like if she hadn't died. How different would he have been? He doubted he would have left home, certainly not at the young age he had. Would he have ended up here? Been here to find Eliza?"

"Ready to go?" Cal cut through his reverie, coming up behind him.

"I'm ready." Matthew looked to Eliza then reached down and picked up his bag.

"I'll be fine," she assured, obviously picking up his reluctance. "I'll see you in a couple days. You listen to Mr. Bartlett. Do what he tells you."

Matthew nodded, hugged her tight then stepped away. "I don't have much experience riding a horse," he said seriously to Cord.

"Well, if you're like your sister, that shouldn't be a problem. She had Rufus here galloping around almost from the minute she got on his back."

"This here is Aspen." Cal motioned to the tall white horse with little black flecks in her coat. "She's as gentle and good tempered as they come. I can shoot a gun from her back and she won't even twitch an ear. She's also as sure-footed as a mountain goat. A right good animal. Had her since I was about your age, so she's getting up there but still sound." Cal rubbed the horse behind her ears.

"Around on this side." Cal positioned Matthew next to the horse. "Now reach up, hold here and here. Good. Pull yourself up."

Cord noticed Hannah watching the process. He'd have to mention to Cal he might want to give her a riding lesson. Interesting form of courting. Beats the thought of sitting in a parlor trying not to stare at the lady.

Matthew settled in the saddle as easy as Eliza had.

"Ready?" He looked at the youth who nodded, excitement showing on his face.

Cord swung up on Rufus and tipped his head at the ladies. "I'll see you about eight o'clock, morning after next."

He waited for Eliza's acknowledgement. The smile that accompanied it was a bit forced but calm. Fear was no longer forefront in her eyes.

He turned his horse letting Matthew move in beside him. "I've never been on a ranch before. Do you have a lot of cows?"

CRED

Eliza watched her brother ride with Cord. Emotions tumbled through her. She couldn't believe Matthew was here, had come all the way on his own. She didn't want to believe Silas might actually be after her and hardly dared believe Cord Bartlett had come to her rescue again. Of all the things she was facing, it seemed the easiest to accept, but the one that made her heart pound the hardest.

"Why don't we go in now?" Amelia slipped an arm around her.

"Ladies," the sheriff acknowledge them all but his eyes drifted to Hannah, who turned and darted through the door.

"Thank you, Sheriff," Eliza said before turning to follow her friend.

"Thank you for cleaning up for me," Eliza said to the women as they entered the room now all set and ready for morning.

"How many times have you stayed and taught me how to do something? Mrs. Burns actually complimented me on my pie crusts yesterday."

"She should have. They were perfect. Flaky. I heard several comments on them," Hannah said.

"Yes, but I did them by myself, without Eliza to help me, and she's the best. Which isn't anything putting them against yours. Your pies are amazing, too."

Hannah laughed. "It's all right. I agree. Eliza has the touch with pies and rolls."

"Your scones and biscuits are better." Eliza joined in the banter.

"And now mine are very acceptable. I can't believe it." Amelia hugged herself. "I can cook – me!"

"You do more than that." Eliza said.

"I know. It's wonderful."

Amelia's exuberance lifted Eliza's spirits and carried her back to the kitchen, where they stopped to dish themselves some leftover stew for the supper they'd missed earlier."

"So you're going to spend your free day at Mr. Bartlett's ranch?" Hannah shared a grin with Amelia.

"That's right," the petite brunette said. "But I believe they were already planning that."

"We were just planning a ride." Eliza felt her face heat and knew it had gone bright pink, just as it had every other occasion they teased her.

"Yes, but he's not invited any of the other ladies for a ride," Amelia said pointedly.

"A fact that extremely annoys Bessie." Satisfaction rang in Hannah's voice.

Eliza took a bite to save herself from saying anything but the strategy failed when each of her friends put a spoon full of stew in their mouths then waited.

Eliza swallowed. "I don't know what to think," Eliza blurted out. "He's been so kind and he's handsome."

"Extremely," Hannah added.

"I get a touch tongue-tied. I've never had that happen to me. Men have always been kind of silly to me. They've made plays for my attention and my hand without even trying to get to know me. It's been hard to take them seriously when there's no way they can be sincere."

The blush flared again. "I've never kissed a man before. I've had a lot try to kiss me but I've always ducked out … I just couldn't let them kiss me. I didn't really feel I knew them enough or wanted to know them. The couple I did feel I might know enough, just felt wrong." She glanced up.

"Don't look at me." Amelia said. "My father would have beaten me if I kissed any man. Not that any would have been interested in me."

"Amelia!" Eliza shook her head as the woman's self-doubt slipped out.

"I've only been kissed by one man. He was the son of one of my employers. As pompous as his father. I didn't want him to kiss me. The other maids had warned me about him."

"Hannah!" Horror spiked in Eliza with concern for her friend.

"No!" Hannah cut her off. "Fortunately that didn't happen, not that I doubt it wouldn't have if I'd remained there," she said shakily then smiled a little. "I kicked him like one of the girls on my first job told me to do. I dropped him to his knees. He fell against a beautiful lyre table, knocking it over, breaking a vase. It made a loud clatter. Everyone came running. They all knew what happened but I was let go for breaking the vase."

"That is so unfair." Amelia protested.

"True, but it happens."

"Still, it is wrong," Amelia finally said, more to sweep the mortification away. "I'm glad you were so smart. How'd you make him drop to the ground?"

"I brought my knee up hard between his legs. I can't believe how effective it was."

"Oh." Amelia blushed.

"Oh is right, but it worked. I'm sure Ambrose never saw it coming."

"It must have been terrifying though." Amelia cringed.

Eliza couldn't help wish she's known about it around Silas. Maybe it would have ended his pursuit of her if she'd done something like that the first time he made an attempt to corner her. "That is all it took?"

"Yes, but do it hard and I'm sure it helps to take them unaware, I think."

"I've never heard of such a thing." Eliza considered it,

"Me either. Though it's not surprising, my father not letting me know."

"One of the grooms taught me how to hit." Hannah

added with a slight hesitation.

"Really?" Amelia got out before Eliza could, bubbling with interest.

"He'd had hopes of being a prize-fighter to make his way," Hannah said.

"He was sweet on you?" Amelia grinned.

"I think more he was sweet on the extra-large servings I would give him." Hannah met her with a grin of her own. "He was a big man and needed it."

"Well, show us how." Amelia's excitement quivered in her voice.

"Make a fist," Hannah said. "Don't put your thumb inside or you'll be apt to break it." Hannah reached out and shifted Amelia's thumb and Eliza copied the placement.

"Now, what he told me to do was, instead of pounding a man, which is what a woman would normally do." Hannah demonstrated. "Try to stay calm, wait for an opening and thrust your fist out putting all your weight into it and go for the nose or eye. John said nose is best."

"Was it common you'd be attacked as a maid?" Eliza asked the thought that struck her.

"I won't say common, but it was heard of. I only had the one incident, but I also tried to be very careful after that. I asked around before accepting a post."

"I'm glad you're here." Eliza wrapped her arms around Hannah. Amelia joined in making it a group hug.

"I never thought I would have friends like you," Hannah said. "Don't get me wrong, it's not like I didn't have friends, but none like you, that I feel so close with."

"Well, I was never allowed to have friends, but I think we're more. I know I can count on you for anything. That makes us sisters," Amelia said.

That brought firm agreements from them all.

"I think it's time to go up now." Hannah stepped back first.

Eliza followed. It had been quite a day. She glanced

across the dining room revealed by the moonlight that streamed through the windows and glistened off the tracks beyond. A shiver skittered its way up her back.

Could Silas Marsh really be headed this way – after her? It seemed impossible, but she couldn't seem to beat the fear down.

With a great amount of effort, she managed to shake off the unease and hurried to keep up. It did no good borrowing trouble. Halfway across the kitchen, the door to the supervisor's room opened. Light silhouetted Mrs. Hyde wearing her nightgown and wrapper.

"Miss Telford, a moment."

The other two women stopped with Eliza.

Mrs. Hyde sent a glare their way before directing her attention. "You have your second warning, Miss Telford."

"Second? For what?" Eliza struggled getting words out past her shock.

"I told you not!" She stressed the word. "To slip your duties onto your friends."

"But –" Eliza come up with an objection.

"She didn't, we –" Hannah started, only to be cut off.

"I suggest you say no more, Miss James, or it will be a warning for you, too. And, I don't believe you can afford that."

Eliza reached over and laid her hand on Hannah's arm, seeing Hannah's retort coming. "It's okay," she whispered. Eliza dipped her head in acknowledgement to the overseer and wordlessly made her way across the room.

"That is so unfair," Amelia said when the door closed, dropping them into shadows, as little outside light made its way inside.

"But there's nothing you can do about it. I think she was hoping you'd react so she'd have cause to give you each a warning."

"I can't believe she lets Bessie get away with her conduct. She's always lax in her work and sluffing it off on others," Amelia whispered as they made their way up to their sleeping quarters.

They reached the top of the stairs just in time for one of Bessie's snide remarks to reach them. "The way he hugged her. If you ask me, he's not her brother at all. I bet he's her son. My brothers never acted like that."

Eliza stepped into the opening, looking down at the woman sitting on her bed. "I presume you are talking about me. If so, I was only nine when Matthew was born, so I hardly believe it would be possible for him to be mine." Eliza stood straight, her tone firm. "As for the way your brothers act, that is sad, but whose fault is that?"

With that, she turned to the other section where her bed was. The small shriek that followed gave her a touch of satisfaction.

"How long do you think it will take her to learn not to antagonize you?" Hannah grinned.

"I don't know, but I'm not going to take it anymore, since it's obvious I will always be found at fault," Eliza answered as she unpinned her hair, letting the lengths drop around her shoulders. "Do you think it was wise of me to let Matthew go with Mr. Bartlett?" She looked at her friends as she ran the brush through the locks.

"The sheriff wasn't concerned. In fact, he was in full agreement," Hannah answered first. "I think, if anyone would know the kind of man Mr. Bartlett was, it would be him."

"They're friends," Eliza pointed out.

"As I said, he'd know." Hannah pulled back the blanket on her bed and picked up her nightgown, stepping behind the screen to change.

Amelia reached across the space between their beds and laid a hand on hers. "What do your instincts tell you?"

Eliza grew warm. "I ..." She stumbled getting the simple word out. She swallowed and tried again. "I feel I can trust him."

"Then do. Trust yourself. If it helps, I think Mr. Bartlett is a good man. I saw how fast he came to your aid that first day. He protected you, but I think he would have done the same for any one of us." Amelia flopped down. "I'm good at reading 'mean' below the surface, just not 'nice' because I haven't spent much time around it. Believe me, I think he is truly kind."

"I agree with her." Hannah stepped out, now changed. "Now relax and go to bed."

While Eliza waited for her turn to change, Hettie, Arlene, and the other girls that share that section came in. They grinned at her but in a friendly manner, letting her know what Bessie said hadn't changed their opinion of her.

"Anyone else going out tonight?" Hettie asked, pulling out a ball of yarn.

"No," Eliza exchanged looks with Hannah.

"Good." Hettie tied the end of the yarn to the leg of the chair that sat by the door. "This is a trick I learned from my brothers who would have hugged me like yours, though they never failed to play tricks on me also."

"What are you doing?" Amelia asked.

"Making a warning trap, in case Bessie tries to sneak in here and do something mean to Eliza." Hettie made it sound obvious.

"Bessie is in a rage," Arlene agreed as Hettie tied the other end of the yarn to a tin cup and placed it so it barely rested on the corner of the basin table on the other side of the entry way.

Eliza felt a touch lighter when she laid back in bed a few minutes later and the room dropped into darkness with the lantern being extinguished. She would be all right. She had friends.

CR80

Cord glanced at the boy riding beside him.

"We should have brought Eliza here," Matthew said for about the hundredth time that day, and it wasn't even noon yet, and that wasn't even counting the evening before, on the way to the ranch. The boy seemed to love it and being outdoors.

The problem was, Cord was in agreement. He'd have felt a lot better if Eliza was there for him to look after. He couldn't say if it was due to the possible threat from her stepfather or his own selfish reasons of just wanting her there, with him, on his ranch.

He glanced again at her brother. "She'll be here tomorrow. She's safe enough in town. There are plenty of people watching after her. Do you think Eliza will like the ranch?" he ventured forth the question that had been on his mind recently.

Matthew beamed. "She'll love it."

Cord wasn't sure if that was the boy's thoughts, the way he'd been following him around all morning, or actually what Eliza would think. Matthew's next sentence gave him more cause to hope.

"I don't think Eliza likes the city much. She prefers the gardens and parks. Being outside."

"What about going to parties and functions?"

"She didn't go much. First after Dad died she didn't go out because of mourning. After that, she only went when she had to. Men were always making a fuss around her, and she didn't like it because they never really talked to her."

Cord wanted to ask what he meant by that, but fortunately Matthew answered before he figured out how to word the question without sounding like he was prying information out of him.

"She said it was like they were hanging on her every word, then they just talked over her like she hadn't said anything. Treated her worse than a child. Like she couldn't possibly think of anything of importance or could be honestly interested in anything that was said."

Cord thought back at how he'd doubted she could be interested in the ranch then remembered how apt her attention had been and probing her questions were. "Eliza has a bright mind."

Matthew nodded. "She likes to learn. It doesn't matter what. We had a tutor that finally told father Eliza had learned everything he could teach her. I think she should be a teacher. I don't know why she didn't think of it when she was looking for a post."

A wash of relief swept over Cord that Eliza hadn't gone to teach or she wouldn't have ended up here.

Chapter Nine

Eliza settled in the chair inside the small garden just off the kitchen then rose and paced across the back of the building, pausing at the door to listen to the bustle of morning preparation going on within. The first train should arrive in about twenty minutes. Cord was due in ten. She'd been ready for thirty.

Her heart fluttered. She tried to convince herself it was just so she could go see Matthew. She didn't want to think it was due to Cord Bartlett, or the chance of spending time with him. He was just a kind man. She said the words in her mind trying to convince herself.

"All ready to go?" The slow easy drawl of the man she was trying not to envision pulled him into fine detail even before she jerked around to face him. The morning sun set him aglow, bringing out the golden streaks in his hair, visible because he held his hat. His large hands were working the brim of his hat as if he might be a touch nervous. Eliza found it an oddly endearing behavior for such a large, confident man.

He waited just at the edge of the porch, which as she approached made them the same height. Eliza was used to looking men straight in the face but, for some reason, it was a little disconcerting looking into Cord Bartlett's eyes. The blue in the gray was a little brighter this morning, picking up hints of the sky. She drifted into them, becoming lost and not really wanting to be rescued.

Eliza didn't know how long she stood staring until the clatter of pans in the kitchen pulled her back to reality.

"Ready?" he repeated. The word rumbled from deep within him as he extended a hand to her.

She nodded, feeling like something more was being asked, especially when his hand enclosed hers.

Together they walked through the alley to where he left the horses tethered. Rufus stood next to a light tan-colored horse.

"This is Lu, short for Lucille. The man I got her from said he named her after his first love. But just like the horse, she got away from him. She's getting up there in years but is still sound and the best riding horse I've got. You can carry a cup of water and never spill a drop."

"I think she's beautiful." She stroked the mare's nose, conscious of him watching her.

"If we put you over here, you can step up on here and on." He motioned to a couple wooden crates.

"Can you teach me how to mount without a mounting block?"

"It might be a little tricky with your dress." He reddened a little, bumping his hat back to brush at a lock of hair over his brow.

Eliza pulled the folds of her skirt out wide so it parted to reveal it was split and sewn down the middle.

"Well I'll be. I never guessed."

"One of the others had a riding outfit I borrowed to see how to reform this. It was my oldest dress, but I think it turned out quite well."

"It did indeed. All right, come here." He angled her to face the horse. "You're going to put your foot in the stirrup, grip here and here. As you pull yourself up, press with your legs in the stirrup, kind of standing up and swing your other leg over."

Eliza pictured what she'd seen, and what he said, and went easily in the saddle. "I did it! She exclaimed unable to contain her excitement.

"You did. Nicely done." He beamed up.

Warmth spread over her. Her heart raced making her breathless. She fought to ignore the reaction, but whenever she got near him it came – actually it came just thinking about him. "How is Matthew?" she said the first thing she could think. "He didn't come with you?"

Cord stepped back. "He went with my foreman out to look at calves. He's been worried about you, but is enjoying the ranch. He's taken to horses as easy as you."

"I'm glad he's enjoying himself. I'm afraid he's going to be disappointed when I have to send him back to his mother, but I can't keep him here. Even if I had a place for him, it wouldn't be fair to her. I just don't know what to do about Silas Marsh." It had always been hard to think of him as her stepfather, now it was impossible.

"We'll think of something." He placed his hand over hers, where it rested on the saddle horn, and gave it a squeeze.

The strength in his hand rushed up her arm right to her heart as did the crooked smile. It lightened her mood. He gave her fingers another squeeze before turning to Rufus and swinging up into the saddle. "We better go. The day's a wasting and your brother will be getting anxious."

He started them out at an easy walk. The warmth of the morning sun gave her a wave of comfort. At least that was what she tried to tell herself. As they went, he told her about who lived in all the places they passed.

Homes grew farther and farther apart. They rode in silence for a ways.

"Would you like to try a gallop?"

Exaltation spiked. "I'd like that very much."

He smiled at her. "Give Lu a nudge with your heels."

The horse moved immediately into a trot that was much smoother than Rufus's had been.

"Nudge her again." His voice came from just behind

her.

She did just as Cord galloped up beside her and Lu matched his pace. The ground flew beneath them, but she felt no fear at Lu's smooth gate. Delight slipped free and she laughed, tipping her face up to the sky. Eliza wished her hair was free so the wind could blow through it.

Cord didn't say anything for which she was grateful as she reveled in the freedom. When he finally slowed, he was grinning as broadly as she knew she was.

"Enjoying yourself?" he asked.

"Oh yes. Nothing has ever been like this."

He let Rufus walk the last couple feet up the small rise they were climbing. He paused at the top, sweeping his arm out in a wide arcing motion. "Well, this is it." He waited for her to comment.

Eliza looked down the rise at the large white house at the bottom and gasped. It was much bigger that she expected. Besides the barn, there were also several other buildings. One she guessed was a bunkhouse. Instead of just one corral, there were three. A pasture dotted with cows and horses stretched out behind it all.

Sitting on the rise the way they were, she could see the same wide stream that flowed into town cut right through the middle of the land, with clusters of trees and bushes growing at different locations along the bank.

"Oh, this is beautiful. No wonder you are so proud of it."

"I admit, it was my dream." He leaned forward, crossing his wrists, resting them on the saddle horn.

"You've worked hard to make it come true."

"You want to go down and have a tour now before Matthew gets back?"

"I'd like that."

C3♥80

Cord brought his horse to a trot, keeping a close eye on the woman beside him. Actually it was hard not to watch

Eliza. Saying she was a beautiful woman was an understatement. She was like the sun kissing the earth after a storm and gracing it with a vibrant rainbow. She was glorious with her smile radiating pleasure. Even the possible dangers she was facing couldn't dim the warmth of her glow.

He couldn't get his mind off her fleeing her home to avoid her stepfather. She should have been cherished and cared for. He respected her fortitude to plan and execute her escape. It took a lot of courage to leave family and the only home you knew.

They closed the distance to his home, the one he'd created for himself. The one that was missing something that until the last couple weeks he couldn't figure out what that something was. Glancing at the woman riding beside him, he wondered how he was ever going to convince her she was who he needed to make his life complete. He cared for her. His mind objected at the weakness of the word 'cared'. Love came to mind, and his first instinct was to brush it away, but like a burr to a saddle-blanket, it clung there.

Swinging down, he came around to help her in the midst of the same action. At his touch, she lost her grip and tumbled back into his arms.

"Easy," he chuckled. "I didn't mean to startle you."

"Oh." She blushed as she used a hand on his chest to steady herself. "Sorry."

"It's all right. I wasn't thinking. It will take a bit of time for you to get used to being in a saddle." It wouldn't take any time to get used to holding her though. She was perfect in his arms. The long length of her meant he wouldn't have to bend in half to kiss her, or get a crick in his neck just to look her in the face.

Remembering her cuddled against him and resting her head on his chest after the attack, he longed to tighten his hold, wishing she would lower her head and nestle into him once more. Lean on him and let him take care of her, but she was an independent little thing. Okay, not so little. She was tall but willowy. So perfect for him.

As if reading his mind, she raised her chin, tipping her head up slightly so she met his gaze. The beautiful morning sky reflected in her eyes. He wanted to see that view every morning of his life.

A sound from the stable had him stepping back before he could follow his inclinations and kiss her. He wouldn't risk damaging Eliza's reputation by doing that. Besides, he wanted her to feel comfortable here. A safe harbor. He didn't know what fears her stepfather had left on her.

He motioned her up the steps before him, then reached around her to open the door, watching her face as she entered. A small parlor, which he never used, sat just to the left. The rich hardwood of the sitting group was padded with a vibrant red material. It looked good, but he couldn't claim to choosing it. It had come with the house. Most of the furniture did except his room.

The bed that was in there was moved to another room because it wasn't long enough to fit him. He'd had a man in town, who did exceptional woodwork, build him one with a dresser and chest to match. They were sturdy, beautiful pieces. Not that he'd be showing them to Eliza.

He stood back and let her look around. Her natural curiosity carried her through the house. She paused a long time in the doorway to his den. His desk had been made by the same man, another excellent piece of work.

Eliza followed the hall down to the big room. There he heard her gasp as she crossed to the window to take in the view. "This is amazing. Just like you said." She looked back at him.

"Wait until you see it in the evening." He stepped forward. "The dining room is there and the kitchen on the other side. I apologize if it's a little messy. I had a housekeeper but she quit to move to California with her daughter last week. I haven't had time to find a new one yet."

"This is a beautiful house."

"There are four bedrooms upstairs. I honestly can't take much credit. The old man that built it made good money mining. He built the house for his mail-order bride, but when she arrived, she took one look at the town and wouldn't stay. That was eight years ago. Things have changed a lot in town since then. He hung onto the ranch but his heart wasn't in it."

Cord looked out, finding the satisfaction he always did. "About two and a half years after that he hired me. Things were getting a might run down. He didn't have much of a herd. He had gone through most of his money, and was alone except for a couple hands that didn't do much if they could get away with it."

She looked up with interest so he continued. "I was his foreman, got things in shape. I bought it from him four years ago. He decided he'd had enough, and his health wasn't good."

"What happened to him?"

"He stayed here. Passed away last fall."

"You built this up. You were so young."

"I'd been a hand about five years by then on several spreads, drifting, trying to find a place that felt like where I wanted to be. I had fourteen cows and a real good bull I raised myself when I got here. I just needed the place and was real fortunate to find the right one.

"You are amazing," she said so softly that if he hadn't been so close, he wouldn't have heard. Once more her head tilted up to look at him.

Cord didn't remember closing in on her and realized they had somehow met in the middle. He felt himself dip into her eyes as he lowered his head. Her lips parted slightly. He wondered if it was a conscious offering, but knew only that it was irresistible.

He lowered his head, feeling the whisper as her breath caught, but she didn't pull back.

"Eliza! You're here." Matthews's voice echoed through the house with the sound of the door opening and closing.

Cord was across the room when the boy entered.

"I can ride a horse. Mr. Bartlett said that I was good. Did he tell you?"

"Just like you were born in the saddle," Cord said. He was unable to take his eyes off Eliza. Her cheeks were flushed a rosy pink that was most becoming. "Your sister is just as good. She galloped most the way here."

Matthew beamed with pride. "Eliza can do anything."

"I'd say she is amazing," Cord agreed. "I was about to take her on a tour of the house. Do you want to do it since you already know your way around?" He honestly couldn't say he welcomed the interruption, but figured it was for the best that they were chaperoned.

"Sure. You saw the front." Matthew motioned and waited for Eliza to react. "Through there is the dining room and the kitchen. It also goes out into the parlor and has backstairs to the upper floor like our house."

"Out back is a garden full of vegetables. You'd like it but it needs weeding. I did some to help out."

Cord arched his brow. He didn't know that.

Matthew turned to him. "Eliza's always trying to grow vegetables back home. She has them mixed in with the flowers. Dad always said she got her practical side from him and her talents from her mother. That's why she can do anything."

Cord followed them upstairs "That's interesting. What are some of her talents besides growing plants?"

"She can sew by just looking at it and it always fits. She takes old things and remakes them so you'd think they're new."

"That's a nice talent."

"Mama says so. Especially with a growing boy around."

Cord laughed, figuring Matthew heard that quite a bit.

"This is my room." Matthew opened the door to a room with pride. "Mr. Bartlett's is down there. I saw into his room. He has the biggest bed I ever saw."

"You shouldn't be poking in his room."

"I wasn't, just the door was open and I could see." Matthew glanced at him, looking sheepish. "Honestly, I didn't poke."

"It's fine. No harm."

"Will you show Eliza?" her brother asked.

"Matthew!" The pink in her cheeks went a whole lot brighter.

Cord couldn't help himself. He reached over and turned the knob, pushing open the door to his room. Fortunately, the bed was made. One task installed in him by his mother.

To give Eliza credit, she tried not to look, but at Matthew's exclamation, she glanced up then stared. "Oh," the sound slipped out. "It's beautiful." She started to take a step forward, caught herself and froze. "We should head out now if we're going to get to see some of the ranch and the lake." She spun and practically flew down the stairs.

Matthew looked confused.

Cord dropped a hand on his shoulder. He almost told him it was all right, he would never understand women, but he could make a good guess at the nicely flustered Miss Eliza. "Come on. She's right, and I'm thinking we need some food to take with us to eat out by the lake."

"All right."

It didn't take much to please Matthew.

ೞೞ

Eliza couldn't believe the enormity of the ranch. No wonder he had so many hands. There was no way one man could handle it all. When she said so, Cord just laughed.

"It's not that big, but I've some good land and stock."

They followed the stream. Breaking through the trees, a lake glistened in the sun.

"It's lovely."

"There's a nice little area over by those trees where we can eat. If you want to swim," he directed to Matthew, "the water will feel real good."

"I'm not a very good swimmer. There wasn't anywhere close to go back home." Matthew looked away, as if embarrassed by the admission.

"Well, I guess that's something we'll have to work on. You never know when it might be necessary, but I'm afraid I didn't come prepared today with your sister here."

"Can I go down to the water still?" Matthew asked.

"Certainly."

"Just remove your shoes and roll up your pants," Eliza added. She'd like to go herself, but it wouldn't be proper.

A few minutes later, she watched Cord pull off his boots to wade in the water with her brother. She reached for the laces of her shoes, hesitated a moment before removing them and her stockings, as the beckoning water and joyous expression on the males' faces won out.

The grin Cord gave her as she joined them was as gratifying as the water. The temperature was perfect as was the soft, silty mud between her toes.

"Eliza." Matthew splashed at her but the water fell short.

"You sure you want to do that?" The splash Cord sent toward Matthew doused him.

Matthew just laughed trying to get him back.

Eliza was laughing when the misdirected wave hit her. "Oh." She laughed harder.

A short time later, they were all soaked and still laughing when they made their way back to where the food waited. The males ate ravenously and Eliza kept pace with them. Nothing had ever tasted so good and the warm sun felt amazing.

Replete, she tipped her head back enjoying the sun on her face. About half her hair had come loose and hung limp around her shoulders. Eliza knew she must look a sight, but at the expression on Matthew's face she didn't care in the least. She removed the pins letting it fall. Running fingers through the mass, she wished she had a brush, but it didn't matter as wet as she was, it wasn't like she looked good. She'd probably be back in town before she was all dry.

She looked up to find Cord watching with an intensity that sparked lightning in his storm cloud eyes.

Once more her cheeks heated. "I know I look a mess, but it was fun."

He stepped toward her raising his hand but stopped just inches from her face. "You look beautiful."

Eliza lost all track of her surroundings.

Cord drew in a breath. "We'd better get back to the house and find you something to wear while your clothes dry, or you'll be uncomfortable all day long. Ready?" He turned to Matthew who Eliza just remembered was there.

"Yes," her brother said with an impish grin.

Eliza wondered what was behind it.

The ride back to Cord's ranch house was definitely not as comfortable in wet clothes, but the air was warm enough to keep it pleasant.

"I don't have any women's apparel," Cord said once they got inside and Matthew went to change. "You can wear some of my clothes though, if you don't mind, that way you won't have to sit around in a blanket until yours dry." He looked slightly embarrassed which Eliza found endearing.

"That would be welcome."

"I'll get them. You can use my room to change, and I'll change down here." He reddened.

"The other room next to Matthew's would be fine," she suggested.

"If you'd be comfortable there." He shifted from side to side.

His thoughtfulness touched her as much as his embarrassment. Who would have thought that Cord Bartlett could get flustered? "I'll be fine."

"Then." He motioned her to the stairs.

She waited outside his room while he got the clothes. At least she was no longer dripping, so she didn't make a mess on his floor. When he appeared with what she figured was his go to church or special occasion clothes, she about told him it wasn't necessary, she could wear anything but at the softness in his eyes she held her tongue.

"Thank you."

"There's a comb there. I'm afraid I don't have a brush."

"The comb is very much appreciated." She took the bundle. "I'm afraid it will take me a while to get through this mess."

He surprised her by picking up a lock and curling it around his finger. "You have beautiful hair, but nothing compared to your eyes, the perfect summer all year round." He pulled back abruptly. "I better leave you to change." He left and closed the door behind him before she got enough breath back that she could begin to answer.

She heard the door close down the hall. Her legs threatened to give way, but she managed not to sink down on the bed. *Had he really said that, or was it just a dream?* She shook her head at the foolishness of her heart.

Removing her sodden clothes was a challenge. His clothes felt odd to her though there was a certain comfort in them. They were huge on her. She had to hold the pants up with one hand as she went downstairs. Her feet clad in a pair of his thick wool socks made no sound.

Cord stood in front of a window staring out, his hand wrapped around a cup. Then, as if he knew she was there, he turned. His lips twitched twice before the grin sprang free.

"Don't laugh," she warned.

Which immediately produced the laughter.

"Do you have a piece of rope I can use to hold up your pants? If I let go..." She cut off and the laughter froze in him but his look blazed with heat.

He stepped by her to the enclosed porch off the back and returned with a length of rope.

"Thank you." She placed the comb on the table so she could wrap the rope around her waist and tie a knot.

When she turned back he was still looking at her. Her heart fluttered as their eyes met.

He cleared his throat. "I have chores to see to." His voice rumbled over her senses. "You can hang your clothes out back on the line on the south side of the house. It gets good sun. Matthew already put his out."

"All right. If you have something I can make it for dinner."

"You don't have to."

"I want to." She cut him off, then blushed. "There is no other way I can repay you."

"That's not necessary, but dinner would be appreciated. There's an ice-house out back. We recently butchered a steer. So pick what you would like." With that, he fled the house like a pack of wolves was nipping at his heels.

Eliza watched him go, more perplexed than ever. She was still staring after him when Matthew entered the room.

"Eliza, you all right?" he said loudly.

"Oh, sorry, what?"

"You were lost in thought."

"Yes, I was." She went over and hugged him.

"You look funny dressed like that."

"Thanks." She squeezed him tight. "I was just going to work on dinner. Would you like to help?"

He nodded.

"Mr. Bartlett said the ice-house was out back, and I saw some promise in the garden earlier when we passed it."

She found a nice piece of meat and got it to cooking before heading to the garden which yielded more than she'd hoped. There were plenty of early green beans that were ready for picking. Matthew showed her the root cellar that still had potatoes and carrots to add to the roast, and some apples she decided to turn into a pie.

"You like Mr. Bartlett, don't you?" Matthew asked while she was snapping the beans.

Her hands stopped in mid-motion. "Yes." She swallowed looking up. "He's a very nice man."

"Eliza." The exasperation in Matthew's voice brought a smile to her face.

"Well, he is."

"Are you going to marry him?"

Eliza barely managed to keep from choking at the shock of the question, followed by the desire it brought. "He hasn't asked."

"But he will. He likes you."

"How do you know that?" She forced her attention back to snapping the rest of the beans

Matthew just stared at her.

When she couldn't stand the silence any longer, she finally answered. "I like him, but I don't know. What would I do if Silas actually does show up? I couldn't stay. Someone could get hurt. Mr. Bartlett could get hurt."

"He'd protect you from Silas."

"I couldn't stand it if Mr. Bartlett got hurt because of me."

"The possibility wouldn't matter to him."

"But it would to me. Also if I married him, I could never go home or be close to you. His home is here and mine would be with him." She didn't mind not moving back to the city, but hated the thought of being away from Matthew.

"I could move here when I'm older." The feelings in the words echoed hers.

"What about your mother?"

Only the crackle in the oven sounded in the silence that hung in the air for a moment.

"I think you should still marry him." Matthew finally said. "You like him."

"Liking isn't enough, I want love." Even as she said the words, she was afraid of the truth. She was already in love with Cord Bartlett, but there was one very big truth – she might put him in danger.

Chapter Ten

Wiping his sleeve over his brow, Cord looked around satisfied with his efforts. He'd thrown himself into work to burn off the pent up desire charging through him like a stallion with its first rider on its back. Because of it, the stables were all mucked out and the repairs done. He even got up the new section on the pen off the main corral. Maybe he should have Eliza out here more often if this was the kind of work he got done when she was here.

His mind went racing back to her just like it always did when he gave it a moment's pause. He wanted to go back to the house, wanted to see Eliza, but just wasn't sure he could. If he hadn't gotten out of the house when he had, he would have kissed her. And it wouldn't have been a gentle, sweet, first kiss type, but the full, claiming type that declared her his.

He didn't know what he was going to do. How he was going to go in and make polite conversation with her in front of her bother, when he wanted to get down on his knee and ask her to marry him? He couldn't believe how easy the thought came, and wondered what she would do if he did.

He knew she found him appealing, at least he thought she did by the way she looked at him. He smiled at the vision of her in his clothes. She certainly wouldn't have thought she was appealing right then, but she was. She was totally adorable in the baggy apparel that hid all of her intriguing curves that were hinted at in her normal dress, and clearly evident when she'd been drenched. Even her hair hanging in damp strands didn't take away from her beauty, just made her beautiful blue eyes appear more striking.

But her looks were not what was so compelling to him. Eliza was courageous, a true friend, and a good sister. She was a hard worker and would stand by him. If she loved him. If she married him.

"We're headed in to eat." Thomas Young, his foreman announced in the doorway. "You joining us tonight?" The spark in his grin said he knew already that wasn't happening.

He'd introduced Eliza to all the men earlier that day. He figured a few still had stars in their eyes and their tongues hanging out.

"Not tonight. Miss Eliza's cooking for her brother and I'm invited to join them." He played it down.

"I wasn't sure if she was still here, not with you being out here working all afternoon."

Cord would have bet the man knew she was still around. It was just his way of saying he was a fool not to be in there with her. He had to agree, but he was trying to hold on to his sanity. "I'm a heading in now."

He stopped at the pump to wash up. The welcoming smell that greeted him at the door was wonderful, but not as good as the woman standing over the stove. His heart filled with pleasure.

Eliza had a towel tied around her trim waist in place of an apron. Instead of her honey wheat hair being piled and pinned on top of her head it hung down her back, tied at her nape with what looked like a napkin or a handkerchief.

"Hi Cord," Matthew greeted him. Cord hadn't even noticed the boy sitting at the table.

Eliza turned and smiled. "Ready to eat?"

"Yes, ma'am."

"If you'll be seated, I'll have it served up. It's all prepared." Color flared on her cheeks. She lowered her eyes making him wonder if it was all from the heat of the oven.

He crossed and picked up the bowl of potatoes she'd just set down.

"You don't –"

"I can help." He cut off her objection. "I've two hands and enough muscle to carry it to the table. At least, that's what my mother used to tell me."

"Oh, where's your mother now?"

"She and my sister died when I was just a little older than Matthew."

"I'm sorry." She looked stricken.

"It was a long time ago, but I try to remember what she taught me. I wouldn't want her to be disappointed."

"I don't think you have to worry about that. She would be proud of the man you are."

Cord straightened a touch. He wanted to believe his mother would think that, and Eliza would too.

At the table, when Matthew went to hold the chair for her, Cord beat him to it. The boy smiled up at him, giving him his acceptance. Cord hoped it was for all things. It felt so right settling down at the table next to her. His only problem was, though he was starved, he had trouble giving the wonderful meal the attention it deserved, when all he wanted to do was look at Eliza.

CB&O

Eliza couldn't remember having a more enjoyable or nerve-wracking dinner in her life. Conversation with Cord flowed with an ease she'd never experienced with any other man. The only problem was her awareness of him, which was something she was totally unfamiliar with. Just his looking at her made her feel warm and tingly all over.

After dinner, Eliza insisted on cleaning up and nothing she said could dissuade Cord from helping along with

Matthew, whose presence made a good buffer. With their help, it didn't take too long.

Eliza excused herself to change and get her runaway feelings back in control. Fortunately, her clothes were completely dry and had come out of their soaking in surprisingly good shape. With her hair once more twisted on the top of her head, she was ready to go. Her steps faltered on the stairs.

She didn't want to leave. She wanted to run back to the room she'd used, close the door and not come out. She wanted to sit in front of the big window and stare out at the hills as the sun set just like Cord had described. She wanted Cord to hold her. The thought should have been shocking to her but it wasn't, not after the way she'd been feeling all afternoon.

She'd just had the most amazing day in her life, but when she closed her eyes and thought of it, the image that came to her mind was Cord.

As if conjuring him, he appeared at the bottom of the stairs.

He watched her descend in silence, jaw locked in some kind of determination.

Her throat went dry.

"You don't look any worse for wear. No one will ever guess you spent the afternoon in men's attire."

She couldn't stop the blush that swept over her. "Where's Matthew?"

"He decided to stay here. One of the mares is about to foal. Thomas moved her to the stable."

"Do you need to stay?"

"I've got time to see you to town. It could be quite a while yet. Maybe not until morning."

Eliza wanted to ask if she could stay and see it, but she had to be at work bright and early. Resigned, she stepped down the last few steps and let him usher her out.

The horses were saddled and waiting. With no way she

could think of delaying, she went straight to the mare and got on, the action quite smooth now. They rode in silence about half the way to town before she spoke.

"I want to thank you for the wonderful day."

"Soaking you in the lake, making you cook for me."

"You didn't make me. I wanted to. It was for my brother too, and I had fun at the lake. It's been a long time since I've had that much fun. I know Matthew did too. He won't want to leave. I can't thank you enough."

"What are you going to do about him?"

"I don't know." Eliza fought down the tears that threatened. "I know I need to send him home to his mother, but how can I with his stepfather there?" It was painful to smile. "And yet, I can't keep him here. I'll know more when I hear from his mother. No message as of yesterday."

"I'll try to ride to town in a couple days to see if you've heard anything. If you need me before that, just send a message. The sheriff will bring one out if needed, but don't worry about Matthew. I'll keep an eye on him, set him to work, and make sure he's fed. Though it will be nothing like tonight. That was a fine meal. I've been missing the cooking with Mrs. Brown gone. She down right spoiled me, I'll admit."

"So what are you going to do?"

"What I've been doing, eat with the men, make it myself, or sneak into town when I can for some good cooking. I can make do with the food, but I'm beginning to miss the laundry and cleaning."

The expression he gave made her laugh, lightening the mood.

"The problem is there aren't many women to hire around here. I hired Mrs. Brown from an advertisement in St. Louis. Her husband had passed on and her daughters had both married and moved away. She was alone, and it was perfect for both of us at the time. That was almost three years ago, then her daughter that moved to California asked her to come. They have room for her now. She was thrilled and I am pleased for her to be around her family. She's wanted it for a while."

"That is nice for her, but so what are you going to do?"

"Not sure. I may see if I can hire one of the town or neighboring women to come once a week. That may work for the time being."

Cord glanced at Eliza wondering if the 'time being' could be until she was his wife. He didn't want her to think he wanted her only as a cook and to clean. He wanted a whole lot more than that or her gratitude. He wanted her love.

With all the turmoil in her life though, how could he get her to see him as more than a friend or a protector? How could he even expect her to want a man's love when she was fighting with the fear brought on by another man?

There was also her job. She'd be contracted to it for nearly another four months, then she could go anywhere. Could he convince her to stay? He decided to think positive. He had four months to win her heart.

"When will you have another free day?"

"About two weeks."

"Would you like to go riding again, even if Matthew's not still here?"

"That would be delightful."

Was there excitement in her voice? She glanced at him, and he saw a spark in her eyes. "I will keep in touch," he said as they rode into town. He didn't want their time to end, but couldn't think of any reason to delay. "I'll bring Matthew to town to visit in a couple days. We can have dinner, then wait until after you clean up so you can spend some time together."

"That would be nice if it's not too much of a bother."

"It's not." The horses came to a stop by the porch. Cord swung down and came around to help her down, not that she needed it. She had the process now.

Silence settled between them as he stared down at her. Her face was tipped up toward him. He imaged it an offering and didn't know quite what to do. He knew what he wanted, but was it considered too soon or too forward to kiss her? He just didn't have much experience with ladies.

He reached up and pulled off his hat, working the brim in his hand to keep from reaching for her. "Good evening." He could swear she blushed. He liked that.

"Good evening. I had a wonderful time."

His lips twitched as the sodden image of her came once more to his mind. Her prim attire clinging to her every curve caused a wave of heat to wash over him.

"I guess you need to get back to your mare?"

He hadn't even thought of the horse since leaving the ranch, which was unusual for him. His ranch and livestock were usually foremost on his mind. "Yes. I guess I should." He let his gaze drift over her face, taking in every fine detail. Her smooth cheeks beckoned his touch but it was her lips that called to him. "I'll see you in a few days."

As if she felt the draw, her head tilted back just a touch more making the perfect angle. He eased in, dipping his head. She didn't pull back. He lowered his head. The sound of approaching voices reached him just before he could close the gap.

He stiffened and stepped back. "Good evening, Miss Eliza." The words rumbled from him as three of the woman came around the corner.

Their chatting ceased at the sight of him, then at once they twittered a greeting and smiled coyly.

"Ladies." He swung into the saddle and turned for home, leading Eliza's horse.

ဃၜ

Eliza tried not to watch him go.

"Eliza," Rebecca said coming up to her. "Was that Mr. Bartlett?"

"Yes. He's letting my brother stay with him."

"I thought he was older, but he's not. He's handsome."
Eliza could understand Rebecca's breathlessness.

"That's why Bessie's drawers are all in a twist. She was going to land him," LuAnn said.

"Not a chance against Eliza," Rebecca said.

"Oh, he's just being kind," Eliza got out, her heart pounding at the thought, still feeling lost in the mist of his eyes. She became aware of the looks she was receiving and tried not to blush like she'd been doing all day. "I better get in and prepare for tomorrow."

It ended up that she was assigned to help with baking in the morning so she had to be up extra early. With that she went straight to bed, not that it did her any good. Her mind continued to replay the moments of the day.

Her thoughts should have been on what she was going to do about Matthew, but all she could think of was Cord. Was it possible to be in love with a man after only spending a couple days around him? Did she even really know him?

Her insides were too much of a jumble to know. When the others came up to bed she feigned sleep, not quite ready to admit the feelings tumbling around inside her.

Eliza's mind, if anything, was even more turbulent in the morning. With rolls raising, she turned her attention to pie crusts, finishing them in time to break down the rolls and put them in the pans.

The time went so fast Eliza couldn't really think about Cord though his image kept flashing through her mind like streaks of lightning, there and gone, sizzling her nerves like being in a thunderstorm. Her pulse quickened.

Was that truly what love was like? She was afraid so. She just didn't know what to do about it. Her life was a muddle and she was tied to her job.

She pulled the last pan of rolls from the oven replacing them with a set of pies. Wiping her brow with her sleeve, she went to replace her work apron with her spotless serving apron before going out in the dining area. It was almost time for the first train.

Bessie glared at her from across the room the way she'd been doing since the moment she stepped through the door the night before. Eliza knew what was brewing on that front, but ignored her to go make sure her tables were in proper order.

A long mournful whistle announced the approaching train. She hurried to fill baskets with the rolls so they would be ready to grab as needed. Steam barely hissed in release of the stopping of the train before the first people hurried in and the rush began.

The first to be fed finished his meal and departed. Eliza was clearing the table when a bulky man slid into the seat next to her. "It will take me just a moment to clear this away and I'll be right with you." She reached for the empty silver roll basket without looking his way.

Thick fingers closed around her wrist.

Eliza gasped, pulling in the familiar cloying smell liberally dosed on to cover the smell of sweat. Terror burned her lungs. Eliza jerked then cried out as the fingers tightened and twisted.

"Just as wanton as ever." Silas Marsh scowled at her from under his brushy eyebrows. "Sashaying around the establishment waving your web of wantonness."

"No." She tried to cry out, but her lungs seized up.

"Let her go!" Hannah demanded.

"Stay out of this. You are certainly no better." The insolent glare he sent to Hannah was enough to break the panic binding Eliza. She picked up the basket with her free hand and brought it down across his knuckles.

A roar burst from him, but he released her. "How dare you?" He sprang to his feet, his hand pulling back to strike.

Hannah's instructions from a couple nights earlier flashed back into her mind. Eliza made a fist and jabbed him in the nose, catching him totally off guard.

Silas stumbled back into the chair behind him, which

fortunately was empty, then crashed to the floor.

Several women screamed. People stood and pulled back.

"Hoyden!" He stared aghast. His chubby face going red. Self-righteous fury sparked in his eyes. "Wait until I get you home. I will teach you proper if I have to beat it into you."

"Leave here? I'm not going anywhere with you and you can't force me." Her voice was steadier then she felt.

"I am your father!" He straightened to look her in the eye.

"You are not my father or even my stepfather." Eliza didn't realize she'd raised her voice until it echoed off the walls. "Now leave," she ordered, standing stiff and unyielding.

To her surprise, he actually pulled himself from the floor, and dusted off his clothes like there might be dirt on them. He sent an angry look her way before he scurried out like the foul vermin he was.

The moment he disappeared, Eliza's knees went weak and she sank down, miraculously ending up on a chair and not the floor. Tremors racked her body, stealing air from her lungs. *He couldn't be here. He couldn't.*

Chapter Eleven

"Ahh." Eliza jumped when a hand touched her arm.
"It's all right," Hannah assured, squeezing lightly.
"He's gone."

"But he'll be back." He was not going to leave her alone. The thought of running away came and went. No matter where or how far she went, he'd follow. Hunt her down. She shivered. There was no use running. Besides, she tried to steady herself, she liked it here. She had friends. She refused to let him rip her away from here like he had her home.

"I need to see to the customers," she said pushing to her feet. Fortunately, all she needed to do was fill tea and coffee. A few minutes later, the first bell rang and people filed out to catch the departing train.

Eliza busied herself in work. Forcing herself to be pleasant, she tried to ignore the looks and speculation in the eyes of the patrons, just as she ignored the glimpses of Marsh lurking in the shadows around the building. When the train pulled away from the platform, Silas Marsh was left standing in broad daylight like a vulture waiting for its next meal.

"Miss Telford."

Eliza jumped, and dropped the silverware she was holding. The clatter echoed through the room drawing attention.

Mrs. Hyde scowled at the floor then up at her. "Pick

those up, then my office." With that, the woman spun and marched away.

Eliza quickly retrieved the silverware and went to follow only to find her way blocked by Bessie, who for once in her life, looked truly pleased.

Not feeling up to the challenge of conflict with her, Eliza shifted going around the other side of the table.

Mrs. Hyde stood at the door of her office waiting. Eliza stepped past her into the room and tried not to flinch as the door was closed firmly behind her. Mrs. Hyde's lips were pinched tight as she moved around her desk. She sat and linked her fingers together with exaggerated care before she looked at her. "I have tried to be patient and understanding with you. Lenient to a fault."

Eliza had to work to keep her mouth from dropping open.

"I've put up with your behavior and your unseemly height, but this is totally unacceptable. A brawl here and you right in the middle. You actually hit the man." Her voice raised with her outrage. "When the sheriff said there might be trouble, I didn't expect any of this. You should have left here two days ago."

"And go where," Eliza broke in. "That man is married to my stepmother. Is living in my house. You saw him, I can't go home. Besides, I am under contract for nearly another four months."

"Not any longer. You are released."

"Released?" Eliza repeated. She knew the woman disliked her and wanted her gone, but this?

"Let go, fired." Mrs. Hyde said forcefully. "I am entirely within my rights to do so. As you just finished your month's pay period four days ago, you are owed nothing more. I expect you to go up, pack and leave. You have not worked enough to cover your train ticket home so you are on your own to get to where you wish to go."

Wish to go. Shocked at what Mrs. Hyde was saying,

she wanted to yell, where would she go? The image of the monster, Silas Marsh, out on the platform haunted her mind. Still, as she looked down on the woman, she stiffened.

"Very well, as it is your decision." Eliza turned, head high and walked out. Tears burned the back of her eyes, but she refused to let them surface. She didn't know what she would do, but one thing was certain, Mrs. Hyde would not see her cry.

Bessie stood in the middle of the kitchen, the gleeful expression still on her face.

Eliza glanced her way then dismissed her.

"Not so high and mighty now. You can forget about Cord Bartlett except to wonder if I got him. Which I'm sure I will, if I decide he's the one I want."

With that, Eliza stopped to face her. "Bessie, I don't have to put up with you any longer, so you might want to keep your mouth shut. I already hit one person today and wouldn't mind hitting another, especially you."

The grin dropped from Bessie's face as she pulled back, obviously seeing the truth in Eliza's eyes.

Eliza sailed past feeling a touch better. It lasted her all the way up to the dormitory room where the first tears slipped free. What was she going to do? Where was she going to go? All she had was two month's pay, and it would take about half of that to get Matthew back home. What kind of job could she get now and how was she going to find one with Silas waiting out there on the street. After his coming all this way, it was a sure bet he wasn't going to leave.

At least, it would be safe for Matthew to go home with Silas here. She just had to get a message to Cord. Bessie's words came back to her. *Forget Cord Bartlett.* She'd never forget him. He … he needed a housekeeper. His had gone to California, and he hadn't gotten around to replacing her.

"Eliza."

She turned at the sound of Hannah's voice and saw Amelia right behind her. Her two best friends in the world rushed to her.

"Are you all right?" Amelia hugged her. "Bessie's saying you were fired."

Eliza shrugged. "Third warning and a major spectacle."

"What are you going to do?" Hannah took her turn for a hug.

"Cord Bartlett," she needed to get back thinking of him that way if he was going to be her employer, "needs a housekeeper. I'm going to ask him for the job."

"But Eliza," Amelia was the first to react. "He's a handsome, single man and you're a beautiful, young woman. It would … people might think." She stopped.

"I don't care what people think. I need a job. He needs a housekeeper. Besides, I trust Mr. Bartlett." She could tell by Amelia's expression that trusting a man was a hard concept for her, but continued on. "I don't believe he would press his attentions on me. I also believe he would protect me from Matthew's stepfather. He's protected me in the past," she added. "And I think he would have his men do the same. I just have to figure out how to get there." Some of the certainty left her voice.

"Are you sure this is what you want to do?" Hannah asked. "Amelia's right. It is tilting what is acceptable."

"You worked in households before," Eliza pointed out.

"Yes, but they've all been older, and I was part of a staff with many others around. Never as a lone housekeeper. I never would have accepted such a post. And you would be the only woman on the ranch, unless one of the other men is married?" She looked hopeful.

"No," Eliza answered. "But it doesn't matter. If he'll hire me, I'll take the position. There's not much choice. Maybe Silas won't be able to find me there."

Amelia looked glum, but nodded. "I don't want you to

leave. Maybe we can at least visit you on our free days."

"I'm sure Mr. Bartlett would allow you to come. Maybe he'll even teach you to ride." Eliza tried for brightness in her voice. "You better get down stairs before Mrs. Hyde gets vexed at you, too."

"I don't care if she did let me go," Amelia said with fire.

"I have half a mind to quit, than what would she do?" Hannah straightened with her hands on her hips. "She would be lacking and have to explain her actions, when she sent out an urgent request for replacements."

"You can't do that. You two need your jobs. I don't think Mr. Bartlett could hire three housekeepers, then maybe I wouldn't get the job." Eliza forced a smile. "I'll be okay. I just need to get packed then find somewhere to hide until dark, then I'll sneak out of town. It won't take me long to walk to Mr. Bartlett ranch."

"Walk?" Amelia said shocked

"Miss Jones, Miss Carrington, if you don't want a warning, you'll get back down to your duties, now." The waspish voice echoed up the stairs.

"Go." Eliza urged. "I'll be all right." Eliza tried to put as much optimism in the words as she could, wishing she truly believed them. She felt totally alone as they disappeared down the stairs.

Surely Mr. Bartlett wouldn't send her away. He was a good man. Look how he took in Matthew, though, she was much more troublesome than her brother. And Silas would make things difficult if he found where she was.

Trying not to think of it, Eliza changed into the riding outfit she'd fashioned and packed her bag. She left her uniforms on the bed to be checked by Mrs. Hyde. As if on cue, the woman appeared in the doorway.

Overly thorough, she went through her inspection. Eliza wasn't offended because she'd done the same on the other two occasions someone left.

"Satisfactory." Mrs. Hyde finally said, then stepped to the side of the room. Eliza took it as her cue to leave. Closing her bag, she picked it up and left the room with the overseer following tight on her heels as if Mrs. Hyde was afraid she might reach back and take the candle from its holder.

At the bottom of the stairs, Eliza paused, not sure which way to go, worried that Silas was still out front or if he had moved to the back to lay in wait.

Rebecca stepped into the kitchen. "Your stepfather is sitting on the bench by the ticket office. We've been keeping watch." She glanced at Mrs. Hyde and picked up a tray of glasses, hurrying back into the dining room.

"Well then," Mrs. Hyde said. "There is nothing holding you back from leaving."

For a moment, Eliza could only gape at the woman, wanting to object or ask how she could be so uncaring. Finally, she shook her head. If she came here in the future, she might say her peace. For now, she sailed through the backdoor with more assurance than she was feeling only to stop short at the sight of the man standing on the porch.

"Sheriff," she exclaimed. Surely, he wasn't there to arrest her. She'd hit Silas, but that was to get him to leave her alone.

"Hannah asked one of the local boys to fetch me. Seems you need help," he said.

"Then I'm not in trouble?"

His lips twitched. "Well, you might be in trouble, but not from what I heard happened. First thing is to get you where you will be safe." He reached out and took her bag. "We'll go through the back alley."

She went with him.

"I should tell you Mr. Marsh stopped by, inquiring about your brother. He wanted to press charges that you kidnapped him." He held up his hand to forestall her retort. "Since I was there right after he arrived and heard all, I told him I knew for a fact that it was an out and out lie. I also told him that Matthew was not with you, but didn't let on that I knew where he was."

"Thank you." Eliza was too choked up to get more out.

"I just wish I could lock him up, but as the law stands, I have nothing to take to the judge."

She nodded. Hopelessness threatened her with tears.

"Hannah said you were going to the Eagle Creek Ranch for a job."

"Eagle Creek? That's Mr. Bartlett's."

"Yes, Ma'am."

"Yes."

He nodded. "Cord will keep you safe, but are you certain? It'll start some folks a cackling like the hen house with a fox in it."

"I can face that."

He stopped and looked at her. "You may not have to, if you're willin'." He said cryptically before he looked around a corner then motioned for her to follow him across the street.

Eliza was surprised when they ended up at the jailhouse. The expression on her face must have been telling because he chuckled.

"Don't worry. Just wait here while I get the horses. Trust me. It's unlikely you'll get any visitors. I'll only be a minute." He was back out the door before she finished raising and lowering her head.

Eliza turned surveying the room. She'd never been to the jail before. A chill ran down her spine, kicking up butterflies in her stomach as she looked at the barred cells in the back of the building. Thankfully, they were empty but for the cots in them.

Eliza paced the floor. She didn't know what she'd do if someone was in one. Still, she turned away. Sun coming through the window reflected off specks of dust in the air, but the room was surprisingly clean. There were a few neat piles on the large desk. The chair behind it had been slid up in its place.

Two more chairs sat against the wall in front of the window. Wanted posters on one wall drew her attention. Most were for robbery, but several were for murder.

She didn't like the thought of Sheriff Steadman going up against men like that. He was a good, kind man, and Hannah was taken with him, even if she wouldn't admit the fact. Eliza also thought he was just as taken with her.

It was obvious from the first time they met, the very day they stepped off the train. Eliza had seen the good-looking man. His lips had been pressed into a serious expression, but he was out to greet people there to stay. He'd been helping people with their bags, then he turned, saw Hannah and froze.

As Hannah had stepped down from the train, her skirt snagged on the handrail, and she was trying to free it while jostling her bag. In a smooth motion, the sheriff had swooped in, knelt and freed her skirt before it tore, and stood plucking her bag from her hand.

She hadn't been sure Hannah wasn't going to hit him and run for a moment. Eliza smiled at the memory, then jumped, ready to do some hitting and running of her own when the door swung open.

Sheriff Steadman stepped inside. "Let's go. I have someone keeping an eye on your stepfather. He's still down the street."

Eliza wanted to yell not to use the term father in any way associated with him, but held her tongue.

The sheriff took her bag and ushered her out, keeping his body between her and the street. His free hand locked on her elbow, but she didn't need any encouragement to hurry.

Two horses waited out back. Eliza recognized the one Matthew had ridden. She went right to it, rubbing its nose and neck a second before taking the reins and pulling herself into the saddle. She was glad she was wearing her riding skirt, and the previous day's riding experience.

They'd barely made it a third of the way when Johnny, a youth that helped at the mercantile, came galloping up. "Sheriff, that man you wanted an eye on." The boy took a breath. "He went to the livery and borrowed a horse. I passed him on the road about a half mile back, about at the Robert's place. He's headed this way."

Eliza caught the hint of an oath muttered by the sheriff. "Thanks Johnny." He looked at her. "That would be your stepfather, if you didn't guess. Someone must have told him where we'd be going, though I can't think of who that might be."

He pushed his hat up as he thought. "Miss Eliza, I know you rode out with Cord. Do you think you can find Eagle Creek on your own?"

"Yes, of course."

"All right, Johnny would you mind letting Miss Eliza borrow your vest and hat?"

"No, sir." The young man said, already taking off his vest.

"Put these on and give me your bonnet." He held out his hand, took the bonnet, and passed it on. "Johnny, you don't have to wear it, but hang it over your shoulder. Miss Eliza, you ride as fast as you can for Cord's. We'll see if we can't get Mr. Marsh to follow us on a wild goose chase."

Eliza donned the vest and hat.

The Sheriff nodded in satisfaction. "That at least hides your hair, which is like a signal light gleaming out here in the sun."

"Thank you," she said to both males. "I'll see your belongings are returned." She directed the comment to the youth. Giving the horse a kick, bringing it to a gallop, then faster to a full out run, she gripped the saddle and leaned low over the horse's neck. Riding all out as if the devil was after her, and as far as she was concerned he was.

She had to get to Cord's. She didn't know when he became parallel to safety to her. Her heart pounded in rhythm with the horse's hooves thundering on the packed ground.

Surely, he wouldn't send her away.

It hit her what the sheriff had said about kidnapping, if Silas found out Matthew was there, he could say that Cord had kidnapped him and force Matthew to be turned over to him. She couldn't let that happen. Silas would hurt him just to get her. They had to get Matthew away from there.

She didn't ease up as she rode over the rise before the ranch. She was half way down the sloop when she heard the call ring out. "Rider coming. Heck of a hurry."

Daniel, one of the men she'd met before, waited in the yard, catching hold of the bridle as she pulled to a stopped almost unseating herself. "Miss Eliza," he said in shocked greeting. "Boss!" he yelled over his shoulder just as Cord stepped out of the barn.

"Eliza." Cord ran across the space separating them, catching her as she dropped from the horse. He steadied her with hands on her arms. "What's wrong?"

"Where's Matthew?" she blurted out. Panic and relief at seeing him warred within her.

"In the barn. What's wrong?" he repeated.

Before she could answer, Matthew appeared in the doorway. Eliza broke free and ran to her brother, hugging him to her.

He squirmed and backed away. "Eliza." He hissed, glancing around, looking embarrassed.

"What wrong?" Cord's question followed her as he had, his hand coming down on her shoulder.

"Silas is in town. He tried to get the sheriff to arrest me for kidnapping you."

"No, Eliza!" Matthew cried out.

"Don't worry. That's not going to happen." She assured him then looked at Cord. "We have to get him out of here. If we don't, Silas will cause problems for you and take Matthew to get to me."

Cord nodded. "Let's get you two inside the house so you won't be seen. Daniel will see to Cal's horse." He ushered them inside not waiting to see the acknowledgement from the man. Once through the door, he plucked the hat from her head and looked at it questioningly.

"It's Johnny's from the mercantile," she said, removing the vest.

He took it and hung it with the hat by the door. "I'll see it returned with the horse. Let's go into the den. I'll get you a drink of water and you can calm down, then we'll talk."

CBEO

Cord took the short cut through the parlor to the kitchen. While Eliza, with her arm around her brother, went the other way straight to the den.

Never had panic hit him like this. Eliza was leaving. He wanted to beg her to stay, to assure her he would keep her safe, but could he? He wanted to say yes. If she'd just trust him, he'd give it his all, but what about Matthew?

Their stepfather could take him and there was no way they could stop him. And if he got Matthew, he could use him to draw Eliza out. There was no doubt she'd do anything to protect him. Which meant to protect her, he'd have to let her go. He couldn't believe the man had come after her.

His stomach tightened along with his fist. He wondered if he could take her somewhere until Silas Marsh left. The men could watch the ranch. The problem was, once again, Matthew.

Cord got the water and headed for the library.

"There's no choice." Eliza's words carried down the

hall. "You have to go. Talk her into sending you to your uncle's."

"But, Eliza."

Cord slipped into the room.

"No. Please Matthew." She cut off his objection. "You have to do this. In fact, it would be best if you talk your mother into going with you. I don't trust Silas."

"What about you?" Matthew cried, and Cord realized Eliza wasn't planning on going with him. Was she staying? Relief rose to plummet at the thought of the danger she'd be in.

"I can't risk leading him back to you. I'm afraid he'll follow me wherever I go. I never thought he would come here. At least, if he's after me, you and your mother will be safe from him."

"You really think you can hide from him?" Matthew asked.

"Yes. It will just make it harder to get messages to you." A tear trickled down her cheek. "I'll have to send them through my friends."

The boy looked solemn. "I don't want to leave you alone."

"She'll be fine." Cord stepped forward, unable to stand back any longer. "She has friends here, and I won't let anything happen to her." It was an easy promise to make.

What he wanted to do was wrap his arms around her and keep her safely here at the ranch. He also wanted to know what happened in town that allowed her to come, but figured now wasn't the time to ask.

"Do I have to leave today?" Matthew asked.

"I'm sorry, yes. The train leaves in a couple hours. It would be for the best. You can make it home on your own?" She waited for his nod. It was slow in coming, but eventually he did.

"Why don't you go up and pack?" She urged her brother out of the room. Once he disappeared up the stairs, she turned back to Cord, her hands clasping and unclasping in front of her. "I have money for his train ticket but I can't take him to town to put him on the train." Tears shined in her eyes, pulling at his heart.

He could feel her pain. "I'll do it." He didn't want to leave her but knew it was more important to her that he be the one to take her brother.

"Thank you." The words rushed from her and her shoulders sagged with relief.

"You're welcome."

"If it would be all right, I would like to make a large meal and pack him enough food to make it all the way there?" The look in her eyes wasn't quite pleading but close.

"Use what you need."

"I can pay—"

She broke off when he scowled at her. "You will not pay me. Take what he needs and make sure it is plenty. Understand?"

"Yes."

He closed the space between them, taking her by her upper arms. "It will be all right. When do you have to be back?"

Her gaze dropped and lip quivered until she bit it.

"Eliza?" He placed his finger under her chin and tipped her head up. The sheen of controlled tears tore at him. They pleaded with him before the question came from her.

"I … I would like to ask you about … the job as your housekeeper."

"What?" His mind tried to shift from the watery eyes to what she was saying.

"I was fired, but I'm a good worker. I can do the job." The words rushed out of her like a dislodged boulder rolling down a hill. "I'm a very good cook, if I do say so myself. I've actually handled much of the running of the house. I even took care of the books after my father died.

I'm quite good if it will help you."

"Eliza." He put his hand over her mouth. He had to stop her, and the only other way he could think of was to kiss her. "Back up. You were let go?"

She nodded.

"Because of your stepfather?" He knew the answer before she nodded again.

She pulled away. "He made a spectacle, and I hit him."

"You hit him?" He smiled at the thought, loving her spunk.

She nodded, picking up a slight grin. "Hannah showed us how. It works very well, but my hand hurts."

He lifted her hand to study it. A slight bruising showed on her knuckles. He brushed his thumb lightly over the area. Hearing an intake of breath, he looked up. Meeting her eyes, he saw no pain then got lost in the blue depths.

She blushed and looked away, breaking contact. "The job," she stammered.

"Eliza, you're a young woman. I'm a single man. People will talk, will wonder."

"That has been pointed out to me, but I don't care. I need a job. I won't go home, so I have nowhere else to go."

He pushed a hand through his hair. "I'm going to say this plainly and not near as delicately as it should be said. I don't want you here as my housekeeper."

She pulled back as if he'd struck her.

He gripped her arms and pulled her back when she would've turned away. "Eliza, I want you here as my wife."

She gasped.

"I know it's soon, but that is what it is. I want you to think about it. I will protect you no matter what you decide, but if you stay here, it will not be as my housekeeper. You may say you don't care about your reputation, but I do. I will not have people wondering about our relationship and the goings on here. So even if you want to wait to consummate the marriage, and I am willing to accept that, but for you to stay here, I will be bringing the preacher back from town with me."

Chapter Twelve

Eliza couldn't take her eyes off him. Cord fairly glared down at her, fire burning in his eyes backed up by what he was saying. Her heart pounded with the words and the meaning behind them.

He'd just asked her to marry him. It wasn't the first time she'd been asked, but it was the first time she wanted to accept. Not that she could. She couldn't force him to marry her just to keep her safe, no matter how tempting it was. But she wanted him to love her like she loved him.

At least, she thought he liked her. Maybe given time, he might grow to love her. *Don't go there.* She couldn't bend to justification, but her mind went right back to it. He was the one that that had suggested it. And he was the one who said they could wait to consummate it. So if he never grew to love her then she could release him.

It might break her heart to do so, but she would because if she left him now, she knew she would be leaving her heart with him.

"Think about it and let me know before I take Matthew to town."

His words jarred her out of her thoughts. "You're taking Matthew?"

"I think it might be better. Don't worry, I'll have the men on guard. You'll be safe here. I need to talk to the sheriff."

"He lent me his horse."

"I noticed."

"He was seeing me here, but Johnny rode out to warn us that Silas was following. The sheriff sent me on, and they were trying to draw him away."

Cord nodded. "Why don't you prepare food for Matthew? I'll go talk to the men." That said, he walked out.

∞

Cord was in the middle of the hall when he stopped and turned back. "Make your decision. Otherwise, we'll have to think of somewhere else for you to stay." He let his anger carry him outside.

The man had actually come for her. He'd wanted to believe Marsh wouldn't, though he'd have traveled a thousand miles for Eliza, but only if she wanted or needed him. Never to threaten or terrorize her. If she didn't want him, he'd let her go. Cord feared it would destroy him, but he'd do it.

He couldn't believe she'd been fired. Just because of the trouble – a spectacle really. It wasn't truly her fault. He couldn't believe it. The women needed to band together for their protection. Most would have stood with Eliza, given the chance. Cord was sure of that, and he knew and trusted all his men to do the right thing.

He headed for the barn as he thought of how he'd asked her to marry him. He groaned. He wouldn't be surprised if she turned him down. He deserved to be turned down. The image of her smiling up breathless, warmth in her eyes, gave him hope.

Cord stopped and looked back. *Please marry me.* He sent a mental plea back toward the house.

Did he see a movement by the window? Could she be watching him? *Please marry me!* He repeated the words in his mind.

It didn't take him long to talk to the four men that were around. Word would be spread to the other two. All were in agreement in wanting to help. Though she'd only been there once, they'd termed her the boss' lady. Cord didn't know how Eliza would feel about that, but for him he prayed it would soon be so.

What if she accepted? Anticipation shot through him only to crash. What if she didn't?

He couldn't let her go off on her own. Even if Marsh didn't find her, she'd be the prey of other men. He'd already seen how easy that could happen on their first meeting.

That made him pause in the middle of running his hand over Delia, a pregnant mare. Was he any better than the other men that wanted her? Was it just her undeniable beauty that attracted him? Yes, he found her beautiful. What man wouldn't? But she was much more. He could get lost in her eyes, her gentle caring heart, her determined fire and strength.

Eliza was a woman who'd stand up for right and those who she cared about. She'd stand beside him in good times and bad. That counted for a lot out here.

She'd work without a whimper, not afraid to get dirty. He appreciated that, too. That was what made him love her. It was who she was.

ᙦᙨ

Eliza busied herself in the kitchen. Her mind still locked on Cords proposal. More than anything she wanted to accept and not because he offered security, but because she wanted to be his wife and love him all the days of her life. She just didn't know if it was the thing to do.

Did he really love her? When he looked at her, she could swear maybe he did but she also got lost in the feelings he created within her at just a glance. Could she really let him marry her, to step in once more to save her? Sacrificing himself, his future, maybe even his life for her.

She could make him a good wife. She was strong. She'd work hard, give him her heart and all she was. Help him, stand by him. Eliza dropped her head in her hands.

She was justifying. Eliza groaned under the weight that he might never love her. For a second she thought he had, when he first started to ask her to marry him. She'd hoped, dreamed it was because he wanted her – loved her.

I'll protect you. Wait to consummate. He didn't want her. Why couldn't the man she wanted want her? She shut her eyes tight, but couldn't hold back the tears. What should she do?

"Eliza."

Eliza looked up to see Matthew standing on the second step of the back stairs. She hadn't heard him come down. Opening her arms, he jumped into them. She hugged him. "I'm going to miss you."

"I don't have to go."

He was volunteering to stay and try to protect her. He'd try just like he did at home, but it would be no use.

"No." Eliza forced a smile and tipped back his head to see his face. "You need to go home to your mother. She needs you."

"But what about you?"

"I will be all right. You heard Mr. Bartlett. He'll protect me. Do you doubt him?"

"No." There was no hesitation.

"I don't either."

"But how can he protect you from all the way out here when you're in town?"

"I'm not going back there to work. I'm going to stay here," she said making it firm in her mind. If Cord Bartlett wanted a real marriage, she would gladly give it to him. If he was just offering to protect her and a marriage of convenience, she'd give him his freedom when the time came, though her heart would remain his.

Sensing Cord, she looked up. He stood in the doorway. His face a mask of stone, not giving out any more of his thoughts than it had when he left.

Please say something, she called out in her mind, but

141

with Matthew there she didn't dare voice her plea aloud. As if reading her thoughts, he glanced down at Matthew then meeting her eyes gave her a nod.

"I moved your satchel to the room upstairs where you changed the other day. Are you ready to eat? We should leave soon."

"Yes." Eliza swallowed and released Matthew after a quick squeeze.

She'd already set the table so started dishing up the food. She started to protest when the males stepped forward to help but quickly acquiesced at a glance from Cord. With their help carrying food to the table, they were sitting down in just a couple minutes. After a blessing, they settled down in silence to consume the meal.

Where the meal at the lake had been a happy light-hearted affair, this time the mood hung like a crushing weight that almost made it impossible for her to swallow. Even Matthew, who was almost impossible to fill picked at his food. They were almost finished when he put down his fork.

"Eliza said she is staying here." He looked directly at Cord.

Her breath caught.

"That isn't proper," Matthew continued. "Eliza isn't married to you," he said seriously.

Eliza choked on her food. "Matthew."

"We will be." Cord ignored her protest, meeting the boy straight on. "My intentions are honorable. I regret you can't be here long enough to witness the ceremony, but you have my word, it will–" Cord stressed the word, "–take place. Right now we must get you away so your stepfather can't use you to hurt her."

Matthew looked thoughtful a second then seemed to accept it.

"Do you have all your belongings packed?" Cord asked.

"Yes. On my bed."

"Good, then if you're ready to go say good-bye to you sister." He turned to her. "I'll get his bag if you want to get the food." He stood leaving them there.

"Are you really going to marry him?" Matthew asked.

"Yes." The word came out easier.

"Good," he said so decisively, she had to smile then it turned into a laugh.

"I take it you approve."

"He's different from the men back home. You never looked at any men like you look at him." His head tilted to the side. "Is that because you love him?"

Eliza took a breath and glanced toward the door Cord had just departed through. "Yes." This time the word was airy with emotion threatening to choke it away.

Matthew beamed. "It will be all right then. I'll talk mother into going to Uncle Jamison's. She won't like it, but she doesn't like Silas anymore either."

Eliza nodded.

"Tell her not to worry about the house and finances. They are in trust. The house is in your name. Have her talk with father's solicitor. Silas can't touch them no matter what he tries. The most he could do is get the monthly allowance. So don't let her let Silas intimidate her into more."

"He's gone through a large portion of her inheritance from her first husband. He didn't know he couldn't get to the other."

"You've been listening at locks." She didn't hold back the grin. Matthew was excellent at learning what was happening. "Tell her not to worry. All is secure. Father saw to it." The thought of her father being gone on top of everything else threatened her with tears.

"Eliza." He stood, coming to her side.

"I'm all right, I'll just miss you." She wrapped her arm around him, laying her head against his shoulder. He was starting to shift into a man.

Tears stung her eyes. Would she see the change? Would she ever see him again? Her throat tightened. She hugged him, then straightened, passing by him before blinking the moisture from her eyes.

"We better get that food. Mr. Bartlett will be waiting." She kept her back to him until she was sure she had herself back under control, then she turned so he could sidle up next to her.

CRBD

Cord watched the pair walk down the hall. Their closeness was heartwarming. He remembered walking like that with his mother.

The image of Eliza with her arm around a boy that looked like a young version of himself came to mind. He liked the picture it made, but in his mind there would be a brilliant smile like the one she'd had at the lake lighting her face. The one she wore now looked brittle and forced. If he didn't miss his guess, there was moisture on her lashes.

He waited silently while they shared one last good-bye then Matthew climbed on Cal's horse. Eliza remained on the porch as they rode out. At the top of the rise Matthew stopped, looked back and waved. She returned it and they continued on.

Matthew remained quiet most of the way to town. So different from their trip to the ranch. He had chattered non-stop. Cord normally liked peace but at the moment he found it disquieting.

"Matthew, are you all right?"

The boy nodded, and the silence continued a full minute more before he spoke. "I know I have to leave, return to my mama, and get her to go to Uncle Jameson's, but I don't want to leave Eliza. You really are going to marry her?"

"Yes," Cord vowed. "As long as she will have me."

"I'm glad. She shouldn't be alone, and not just because

Silas frightens her." He paused. "Just because she shouldn't."

Cord had problems getting past Silas frightening her. He still couldn't believe the man coming all this way.

"Matthew are you sure …" He didn't know how to ask. "Are you sure Marsh never hurt her?"

"No, he never. But he wanted to. She knew it, and I knew it. It was getting harder to protect her from him."

"I don't know why he'd want to hurt her. When he first came, he used to watch her. He was always saying things like it was Eliza's fault, but Eliza's nice to everyone. Even those men who made fools of themselves around her."

"Where there men?" Cord couldn't help ask.

Matthew nodded.

Cord swallowed his reaction down. "And she didn't love any of them."

"No."

He wanted to pry further. He hadn't got any more information than she had divulged previously, but just couldn't bring himself to probe deeper. At least he was sure Eliza wasn't pining away for any other man. Matthew would certainly know if she was.

Silence settled around them until they reached the outskirts of town.

"This way." Cord angled them away from the main road onto a small trail that curved off. "We'll go around the edge of town. I'm going to leave you with a friend while I go get your train ticket."

Matthew followed him without question, stopping and dismounting when he did. The door to the house opened.

"Cord, what brings you here?" A plump older woman came out of the house.

"Good day, Margaret. This is Matthew. He needs a place to stay while I get a train ticket for him. Do you mind if he stays here with you for a while?"

"Certainly, he's more than welcome."

"He needs to stay inside, out of sight." That got a start from the woman, but she didn't hesitate or question. "This way." She extended her arm out to him.

Cord followed them to the door. "I won't be long. I'll get the ticket then drop your horse at the sheriff's office then be back for you, so we can get you on the train just before it pulls out."

Matthew nodded. His body held tight, his expression solemn.

Cord set a hand on his shoulder. "It will be all right. Don't worry, just wait here." He gave Matthew's shoulder a squeeze. "Go on in now, I won't be gone long."

He left his horse there, mounting the other and rode through town back to the train station. It didn't take long to purchase the ticket. Not seeing Cal on the street, he headed for the jail hoping he'd be there.

Cal stood by his desk. Cord realized he didn't think he'd ever seen him sitting behind it.

"I didn't expect to see you in town." Cal said in greeting then tensed. "Did Miss Eliza get there? Is there a problem?" he asked as if answering his question first. "I was sure you'd want her there to protect her."

"She got there and I do, but I'm putting her brother on the train. He's waiting at Margaret's so his stepfather can't get him."

"And use him to draw her out. Makes sense. She'd give herself over to protect him."

"Exactly."

"The man's obsessed. He followed me all the way out to the Grangers, then we lost him. He's not as good a rider as Miss Eliza and sure couldn't keep up with Johnny and me. He finally rode back in to town about twenty minutes ago, went to the hotel by the station."

"Can you keep an eye on him while I get Matthew on the train?"

"Yes. What are you going to do about her? She thought

you might hire her for your housekeeper." Amusement showed on his face.

"That is not going to be, and you know it."

"So." Cal drew the word out.

"I'm taking the preacher back. Want to come?"

A grin spread over the man's face. "I'd be happy to stand up for you, or better yet, give her away since I pretty much handed her to you. She amenable with this?"

"She is but nothing will happen until I'm certain."

Cal arched an eyebrow, but before anything could be said a board creaked out front. A shadow passed over the window just as the door swung open. A man filled the entryway.

He wasn't near as tall as Cord or Cal but easily outweighed them, and it was not all fat. With a ruddy complexion, heavy jowls, and a scowl, Cord knew immediately who he was. There was also something about the man that he didn't like or trust that would be there even if he didn't know what he was trying to do to Eliza.

"Mr. Marsh." Cal's clipped greeting confirmed it.

"Sheriff." The man glared. "I want to know where my daughter is."

Cord realized he didn't notice him and eased farther into the corner behind him.

"I didn't take her anywhere."

"She rode out of town with you. I'm sure it was her on that horse, though where she learned to ride I can't fathom."

"Miss Eliza did ride out with me. She was leaving town."

"She wouldn't have left, not without her stepbrother. Have you found my stepson?"

It hit Cord that Marsh referred to Eliza as his daughter, while Matthew he added step to it.

"I haven't seen the boy since a couple days ago, right after he got off the train." Cord was impressed how Cal told the truth without telling Marsh anything. "He was eating over with Eliza. She was quite concerned that he would come all this way on his own. Do know why he would do that, leaving his mother at his age?"

"I am certain Eliza drew him here. That's why I came after him. They both need to return home. Their mother is quite disturbed. She is of fragile nerves. Eliza is of the same nerves. It is for her own good. She needs guidance."

Cord didn't like what he felt coming off the man, but managed to remain quiet.

"She seemed to do well on her own, at least until this morning. After what happened, she was let go and left town. Said she needed to find a new job."

Marsh continued to glare at Cal for a long minute then turned abruptly, that was when he saw him. Marsh's eyes widened. Slowly, he ran his gaze over him, taking in his height. He scowled and stiffened. "Pardon me." He hurried out the door.

"I'll watch him." Cal came around his desk. "The train should be here any minute. If he heads that way, I'll try to waylay him, give you as much time as possible to get Matthew stowed aboard. I'd tell him to keep out of sight until the train leaves."

"I appreciate it." Cord reached for the door, the train whistle sounded just as it opened.

They headed out going in opposite directions. Cord took a roundabout way, keeping an eye out for Marsh. The man didn't show. The door opened immediately when he knocked. Matthew stood across the room looking nervous.

"All ready." Cord added a cheerfulness to his voice to overcut the tension, hoping to ease Matthew's mind.

Nodding, Matthew hurried forward.

"Thank you, Margaret," Cord said.

"Thank you, Mrs. Dawson." Matthew followed.

"You're welcome. You have a good trip. Such an exciting adventure, but you be careful."

"I will, ma'am." Matthew picked up his bag.

The woman followed them out into the yard.

Cord nodded to her then placed his hand on Matthew's shoulder. "Stay right by me. Wait and follow my lead."

They stayed to the back of the houses, following the same path they'd come in on. When they reached open ground, Cord held Matthew back until he made sure it was clear.

There were only a few people on the train platform when they approached. Instead of mounting it, they moved through the brush toward the back of the train. The warning whistle blew as they dodged across the tracks and entered the caboose from the far side. They went up through the cars with Cord blocking the view of anyone looking in from the platform until they reached the storage car.

"Stay here until the train gets going, then you can find a place to sit." He handed him his ticket. "You'll be all right."

"Yes, I'll find a family to sit with. That's what I did on the way here."

"Good. I'll wire your mother to expect you."

"You'll take care of Eliza?" The boy's concern still evident.

"You have my word." He could hear the engine building up steam. The conductor called out for boarding. He was surprised when Matthew suddenly wrapped his arms around his waist and hugged him tight before releasing him.

Cord patted his shoulder. "Take care. We'll see you."

He left knowing there was a chance he never would, but with trains you never knew. It wasn't like it used to be, and if Eliza had her heart set on it sometime in the future, maybe they'd go. He couldn't say he liked cities, but he'd take her.

Cutting back through the cars to the end of the train, Cord was just about ready to step off when Silas Marsh thundered onto the platform puffing air and looking annoyed. Cal wasn't far behind him and in line to cut him off. Cord caught his friend's attention, and it only took a nod to have Cal shift away.

Marsh stepped on the train and Cord stepped down going straight to Cal. "Matthew's hiding in the baggage car. He won't come out until they're away."

Together they watched through the windows as Marsh lumbered his way through the cars. He made it to the end having to jump down as the train began to move. The satisfied look on the man's face changed when he saw them.

Marsh approached Cal. "Sheriff, what are you doing here?"

"My town. I'm here to ensure peace. Remember, I heard you had a problem earlier here today."

Silas Marsh looked between them then turned and stalked off.

"He's not going to give up," Cal frowned.

"No." Cord watched the receding form.

"What'cha going to do?"

"Stop and get the preacher, then head home. You still want to come?"

"Wouldn't miss it. You really think Miss Eliza will actually go through with marrying you?" His lips twitched.

"I guess I'll find out if she says 'I do' when the time comes."

Cal laughed. "I'm interested to see if it works. I might have to give it a try."

"Does Hannah have a loco stepfather?"

"From what I understand, she doesn't have any family at all."

"Tough luck."

"I'll just have to think of something else."

Chapter Thirteen

Once more Eliza watched out the window, hoping to see Cord come over the rise. There was still no sign of Cord, Mr. Bartlett. The train would have pulled out an hour earlier. What could be taking so long? She had been through the whole house dusting and polishing.

The curtain fluttered in the gentle breeze let in through the open window. She reached out to pull it aside then stayed her hand. Had there been problems? Had Silas got Matthew? Turning from the window, she paced the room, clasping her hands together. She should have gone with him. No, that would have caused more problems. Cord would see him safe. Eliza glanced at the window. Why wasn't he back?

She fidgeted with the chimney of a lamp she'd already cleaned. Taking a deep breath, she tried to bring herself under control. Everything was all right. He probably had business to take care of since he was in town. She should have asked.

She looked around the room, trying to take calm from it. It was a nice room, quite pretty but could use a few touches. She could make some pillows and doilies. Eliza froze, thinking of it as hers.

If Cord actually brought back the preacher it would be. Her heart pounded and it wasn't from fear. She could be married to him by evening. Yes, that made her nervous, but something about the thought was very right. Eliza couldn't imagine giving herself to any other man.

The sound of horses pulling up out front had her rushing back to the window. At the sight of the three men, her heart quickened. Cord, the sheriff and Preacher Evans. He'd really brought the preacher.

Eliza looked down at her dusty riding attire she hadn't bothered to change out of when she started into her cleaning and groaned. She was a mess. She should've taken time to clean up. She'd just been too nervous to think about it.

She wasn't sure if she believed the possibility was true, that he would marry her, just to keep her safe. Eliza wished she could believe it was because he wanted to. She couldn't contemplate it any further as the men stepped onto the porch and through the door.

His gaze went right to her, and he smiled. "It's all right, he got safely away."

She sighed, feeling suddenly weak. "Thank you." Eliza blinked back tears that threatened to spill free and cleared her throat. "Can I get you gentlemen something?" Fingering her skirt, she realized she'd forgot to put on an apron, not that it mattered, she was already dusty from her ride there.

"I'll take care of it." Cord headed for the back of the house with the sheriff following before she could react, leaving her alone with the preacher.

"I asked Mr. Bartlett to give us a minute," the man said without preamble. "Shall we have a seat?"

"Yes, of course. I'm sorry." Eliza settled on the settee so the man could be seated. "I'm a little rattled and unnerved today."

"I understand. Mr. Bartlett told me some of what has happened. That was why I wanted to speak with you, to make certain you do not feel pressed into a union with him. Though he has assured me he will not force … attentions on you, so if the time came there could be an annulment.

You are both members of my congregation, though I don't see Mr. Bartlett often living way out here, you are both my concern. I want to know you are in full agreement."

Eliza nodded, unable to find her voice. Cord had told the preacher everything, even that they would not consummate the marriage. That meant the sheriff also probably knew that he was marrying her to keep her safe, not because he wanted her.

She couldn't breathe, wanted to cry but blinked the tears away.

"You are in agreement then?" he asked again.

"Yes," she managed to get out this time.

He studied her a moment, as if making up his mind. "Very well then. I am pleased to marry you both."

Eliza looked down at the hands clasped on her lap, noticing the smudges of dirt. "Would it be all right if I went up and changed? I won't be long," she assured.

"Certainly, take all the time you like. I'll just let Mr. Bartlett know."

Eliza excused herself and made her way upstairs. Closing the door behind her, she leaned back against it and tried to calm the trembling that had overtaken her. It was a full minute before she blew out a breath and went to her satchel, removing her best dress. She shook it out, wishing she'd taken it out earlier, still it wasn't too wrinkled. She ran her hands down over it to smooth it some.

Fortunately, in her cleaning, she'd filled all the pitchers with fresh water and it had time to warm to at least room temperature. Spurred into action, she quickly washed her hands and face, donned her fresh dress then took a moment to re-pin her hair in a more graceful style that left a few artful wisps framing her face.

Gazing in the mirror, the affect was pleasing, at least she hoped Cord would find it so. Her color was a bit too high, and her eyes seemed a bit too large. She was nervous. She was actually going to marry a man she'd barely known a month. No, she was going to marry Cord Bartlett. Steadying herself, she headed downstairs. The sound of voices led her to the back of the house to the big room.

The number of men had risen to nine. All Cord's hands stood in a group talking with the other men. All showed signs of having washed up. Several had on what was obviously their go to town shirt, most had damp hair that looked freshly combed.

Cord had changed clothes and added a string tie. He looked handsome. Butterflies fluttered in her stomach. She really was going to marry him. He looked up and she lost all thought.

The room fell silent. He stepped to her. "I hope you don't mind?" he asked softly. "I wanted witnesses. I'm sorry your friends couldn't be with you. I didn't think when I was in town."

"Mrs. Hyde wouldn't have let them come." She managed to get out. A pang of sadness hit, but she knew it was true, just as she knew if they could've, they'd have been there for her, even if it meant endangering their jobs.

"It also might have been risky."

She knew he referred to Silas hearing where she was. That was probably part of all the men being there. Cord wanted to let them know she had a place here, not that she doubted they would have protected her anyway.

"If you're ready we can move into the parlor. It's more formal in there."

It was funny, she thought he looked a touch nervous. He also looked right with the view of the mountains behind him. "Actually, here in front of the window is lovely."

He glanced out the window. A smile of contentment slipped over him. Taking her hand, he led her to stand in front of the window, so they were framed with his land stretching out behind. The sheriff moved to Cord's side, while the other men formed a half circle behind the preacher.

It was an impressive scene, but from the moment she glanced at Cord, she couldn't take her eyes away from him. Cord, her husband. She would stand by him and love him, because for her there would never be another.

The preacher's words floated around her like a dream. She hardly registered the question before she heard Cord's deep voice rumble, "I do."

Her answer, when asked, came easily, fainter though full of feeling. "I do."

"I now pronounce you man and wife. You may kiss the bride."

Cord closed in on her. Releasing one of the hands he held, he very slowly slid his arm around her and drew her close.

Her heart thundered then stopped as his lips brushed over hers. The contact was light, brief then gone. Just a taste, and a tingling of pleasure that remained with a longing for more, and a promise for what was to come.

Eliza became aware of the congratulations and teasing of the men going on around her. Cord had eased back some, but fortunately his arm remained around her because she wasn't sure she could stand on her own.

It took a moment for her to gather her wits and to comprehend she was now the hostess there. "Can I offer all you gentlemen a piece of strawberry rhubarb pie? It's fresh."

"Yes, ma'am." The chorus rose from all.

"That's why it smells so good in here," Cord said. "Sure you have enough?"

"I made two. I was going to take one out to the bunk house to say thank you for looking after Matthew. I didn't know what else to do, and there was plenty of rhubarb and some strawberries in the garden."

"Mrs. Brown worked to keep the deer out of them," Cord said.

"And an occasional cow," Mr. Young added.

"The last one that got in there we had for dinner," one of the other men said bringing a round of laughter.

"I'll remember that." Eliza went to get the pies.

She was barely back through the door when they were taken from her hands and put on the table. The action was repeated with the plates and forks. The men circled around with Cord by her side as she served up. It dawned on her, odd as it was, they were Cord's family and now hers.

As if to prove it, along with compliments and congratulations, several oaths were given if she needed anything to just holler. With that the men filed out. The last to depart were the preacher and sheriff. Cord led her out to the horses to see them off.

"Sheriff," she spoke up as the man reached for his reins. "Would you mind stopping and assuring Hannah and Amelia that I'm all right and that I wish they could have been here?"

"I will, but they'll understand the necessity of the timing."

"Yes, still, thank you." She suddenly felt awkward, glancing at Cord. He was her husband now.

Cord shook hands with the men and they watched them ride off.

"I need to go out to the barn." Cord said suddenly, surprising her.

Eliza wasn't sure what she should expect but not that he'd leave her. Evening was coming. One of the men had already taken care of his horse.

She managed a nod. "I'll heat up some dinner."

"That's not necessary. The pie was mighty good."

"Thank you, but you need more than that."

He shifted away, not looking at her. "I don't know how long I'll be."

"I'll have it ready."

"Don't wait. If you're hungry." She got the feeling he wouldn't be in. As if to prove it, he walked away like a fire was nipping at his heels.

Eliza was left to stare after him. Well, she had the question she debated earlier answered. No matter what his kiss evoked in her, Cord really didn't want to marry. In fact, he obviously didn't even want to be around her. He'd only married her to keep her safe.

It was noble of him but she really wished he hadn't. Her heart fractured. A sob snuck out as she tried to steady herself.

Tomorrow, she'd leave. Head to the next town, see what she needed to have the marriage annulled, then she'd go somewhere new. Maybe to California. Anywhere she had enough money to take her to. Women were wanted all over the west. She'd find a man looking for a bride.

It didn't really matter if he didn't love her. It just mattered that she'd never have to see Cord or feel this pain again. Swallowing hard, she went in to warm him some food. Two hours later she returned her plate to the cupboard, leaving his on the table and went up to the room she used.

She stopped to light the lamp. It had been dark outside for some time. There was no light in the barn but the bunk house was all lit up. Mortified, she wondered if Cord was there, that he wouldn't even come sleep in his house with her there.

"I guess then there will be no doubts that he'd touched me." Her words ripped at her as she muttered them.

She glanced out the window into the darkness. It was fool hardy to leave at night but she couldn't stay there knowing he truly didn't want her. Eliza bit her lip to keep back the sob that burned to break free. If she let one tear out she'd never be able to stop. Dark or not, she couldn't wait for morning. She really couldn't stay.

Moisture collected in her eyes as she looked at the satchel on the bed. It was a good thing she hadn't unpacked it yet, but first she needed to change once again. Donning her riding outfit helped get herself back under control.

Taking her satchel, she made her way down the back stairs. She paused in the kitchen and thought of taking some food knowing Cord wouldn't mind, but it was a little too close to stealing. She really should write him a letter, but there was no way she could get cohesive words past the jumble in her heart. She'd just have to wait and send him an explanation along with the annulment. Brushing back the tears that could no longer be stopped, she made her way out the backdoor.

The quarter moon gave light to the land stretching out in front of her. A single mournful moo drifted from the meadow expressing how she felt – alone and empty like the pain that echoed deep in her heart. A warm breeze crossed the meadow to caress her cheek, but did nothing to smooth the chill in her.

It was so beautiful.

I don't belong here. The words shouted in her mind. *It's where I want to be.* She couldn't deny the second thought or the wish behind it. She wanted more than anything to belong there, to belong to Cord.

She swallowed back tears, crossed the porch.

"Don't go far from the house."

A squeak escaped as she managed to muffle her cry. She swung around to face Cord cloaked in shadows, leaning back against the house. Her bag thumped her leg.

Silence filled the air. Even the night sounds froze.

"Where do you think you're going?"

His words set her in motion. She turned and fled, jumping from the porch. Her skirt tangled around her legs, threatening to trip her up. The pounding of footfalls behind her thudded into her heart. She dropped her satchel and grabbed at her skirts, pulling them out of her way not that it did any good. She only made two more steps when an arm wrapped around her waist and hauled her back against a rock hard body.

"No." Agony escaped her as she was pulled around. A hand came up to brush her cheek in a tender motion that totally undid her.

She looked up only to freeze as moonlight crossed his face, highlighting the fury that burned in him. "Where do you think you're going?" The harsh words were so opposite from his touch that they robbed her of the ability to get anything out.

"Where?" he barked.

"I ... away," she managed.

"No." It sounded like pure anguish.

It shocked her and she shook her head trying to clear her thoughts, muddled once more by his presence. "I can't stay here." She finally managed to get out.

"I haven't ... I won't ask anything of you."

The declaration tightened the bands constricting her throat. "You ... don't ... want ... me." She had to force the words out through her shriveling feelings. The weight of the darkness fell on her, crushing her down. Unable to hold back, a sob tore from deep within her.

Eliza pulled back, broke free and fled. For the first few steps only moonlight chased her then once more heavy footfalls thundered with her heart. Tears of pain and humiliation flood her eyes, hampering her vision.

She only made a few more steps before she was caught again and whipped around to face him. A gasp escaped her only to be caught by his mouth. He drank it in and devoured her protest. The kiss deepened, rending her soul and claiming every recess of her then softened, filling every crevasse with his essence – soothing every pain, pulling every response she didn't know she knew how to answer.

A growl rumbled from deep within him as he tore his mouth away. His head dipped down to rest on her forehead. Eliza couldn't do more than bring air filled with the scent of him into her body.

"Did that feel like I don't want you?" he said between

ragged breaths of his own. "I think I fell in love with you the first moment I saw you. I've known for sure I loved you since I cradled you in my arms and you did that cute little rub of your cheek on my chest and into my heart. You claimed me then."

"But–" Was all Eliza managed to get out before he cut her off.

"I figured I had to wait, you were contracted for five more months. It would have given me time to court you then all this happened, but I wanted you to still have time. So maybe, you could start to love me."

"I do love you." The words burst free. "I think I fell in love with you that first day. But the day when you let me ride Rufus and you lifted me down from him. I–"

He kissed her again, long and deep. When his lips feathered free from her lips to run along her cheek, she rested into him.

"I love you."

"And, I love you." He echoed the words with a soft, rumbly whisper.

He encircled her in his arms holding her tight. His heart thundered in her ear. Her heart picked up and matched the rhythm as Cord's lips returned to her mouth in gentle, tutoring kisses.

She whimpered when he broke away.

He smiled down and kissed the tip of her nose. "Will you be my wife forever?"

"Yes." The word carried all her love with it. The true vow that sealed them together. She gasped as he lifted her in his arms and turned for the house. Nervous anticipation replaced the confusion and pain she'd been experiencing. "Cord."

He looked down at her, not breaking his stride.

She swallowed. "Today, at the ceremony was the first time I ever ... kissed a man."

His smile softened. "Did you like it?"

"Yes." She felt face flush.

"I'm glad. I hope you like what comes next."

"As long as it's you."

He froze. "Always." He kissed her again with strong promise pouring through before stepping on to the porch and into their home and life together.

Chapter Fourteen

Light streamed through the curtains tugging Eliza from sleep. The room she opened her eyes to was unfamiliar, but the scent that filled her wasn't.

Cord.

As if picking up his name, the arm draped across her waist tightened, drawing her snug against him. His lips grazed across her neck setting off delicious shivers running through her body. A small moan slipped free.

She felt his lips pull up in a smile, then he shifted them so Eliza found herself looking up into his intriguing gray-blue eyes. There was nothing cold about them now as he leaned over her.

"Good morning, Mrs. Bartlett." His voice was husky, and like his eyes, filled with warmth.

Joy like she'd never known flooded her. "Good morning, Mr. Bartlett." Unable to resist, she reached up and fingered the stubble on his cheek that was a couple shades darker than his hair. It was an amazing sensation.

He turned his head and kissed her fingers. "You have me behind schedule. I'm usually up, dressed and working by now."

"I'm sorry." She couldn't keep back the smile that announced her to be totally unrepentant.

"Are you happy?"

"Very." This time it was pure truth that came out. "But I think we left my satchel outside."

"I'll get it." He lowered his head. "Later." The last word slipped from his mouth just as it closed over hers.

CRRO

They lingered over breakfast. Something Eliza didn't think Cord did very often, then he settled in his den to do paperwork. After his sixth trip out, she realized he was checking on her. Since she was only in the kitchen doing some baking, she decided to approach him about it. Eliza couldn't let him ignore what he needed to do just to watch over her. She was safe here.

She was kneading bread dough the next time he appeared. Coming up behind and sliding his arms around her, he kissed her neck making her forgot for a moment what she wanted to say. "Umm." The contentment poured free.

"You know, I didn't want you for my wife just to have you work for me all day."

She leaned back against him, her hands stretched out in front covered in flour. "It isn't even noon yet, and this is part of what I can do to help you." She suppressed a groan when his lips found an especially sensitive spot just below her ear.

"Do you like that?"

"Yes," she purred.

"I'll have to remember."

"Do, but Cord, you don't have to keep an eye on me. I know you have work to do."

"I am doing work." He didn't try to deny what she guessed. "You just keep distracting me."

"I've just been in here."

"Exactly, you're here in my—our house. I like knowing you're here."

"You're keeping an eye on me, but it's not necessary. There's no way Silas can know I'm here." She turned in his arms, hands held up and away. "Hannah, Amelia, the sheriff and the preacher are the only ones that know where

I am, and none of them will tell. Go out and do what you need. When I get the loaves in the pans, I'll walk out."

"Promise?" He stared down, obviously vacillating.

"Yes. With all that happened, I forgot about the new foal. I presume it came?"

He relaxed slightly. "It did. A little filly. Your brother named her Liberty."

She laughed. "I wonder why?"

"I guess he liked it here. Said you were free here and she was such a sweet little thing."

She laughed again. "He did like it here. You made it wonderful for him." Tears threatened to surface. "He's going to be at his mother's wanting to come back as soon as he gets home."

"At the least, he'll be wanting his own horse."

She nodded as a tear broke free.

"Easy." He drew her to him.

"I'll get flour on you," she murmured as she sank against his chest.

"I'll risk it." He held her tight.

Eliza sighed into him. "I'm usually not as emotional as I've been lately."

"There has been a lot happening."

"I usually handle it."

"You've been carrying everything on your shoulders for a long time. Now you have someone to share the load with." He kissed her temple and nuzzled her cheek.

She sank deeper into him, rubbing her cheek on the shoulder he offered. He had great shoulders.

He cleared his throat. "So how against horses is your stepmother?"

"Quite, but deep inside, she's also a very reasonable woman."

"How'd she end up with Silas Marsh then?"

Eliza pulled back, taking a deep breath to bring herself back in control. "She was still mourning my father. I think she was afraid of being alone and thought Matthew needed a man's hand. Her first husband was a good man. My father was a good man. I don't think she suspected different and Silas put up a very convincing facade."

"But he didn't fool you."

Eliza couldn't suppress a shudder.

Cord's arms tightened.

"He made me nervous."

"From the start?"

She nodded, leaning in to lay her head on his shoulder. "The way he looked at me. Not long after they were married and he moved in, he started in with comments like how pretty I was, to 'what a beautiful daughter I have'. After about a month, it changed to comments about other men watching me. After the third request for my hand came, he started to get more accusatory, 'that I was leading them on'."

She blew out a breath to release some of the tightness in her chest. "I tried to disagree. That I was chaperoned everywhere I went and didn't leave the house that much because I was still mourning my father, but that just seemed to aggravate him more."

A shudder snuck up on her. "Then one night, I was in the den on my own working on the family books, when he returned from an evening out drinking. He started in on the normal—how beautiful I was but quickly changed to calling me a temptress, leading men astray." She bit her lip, then blew out a breath before continuing.

"I decided it best to get out of there, but he cut me off by the door. He grabbed me and tried to pull me to him, but he was drunk. When I pushed, he fell, and I was able to flee to my room. I locked the door."

"You were terrified." His hands moved up and down her arms soothingly.

She nodded. "A while later, I heard the door handle rattle. I didn't sleep at all that night. After that, I kept my door locked. And when he was home, I made sure I wasn't alone. Matthew figured out something was wrong and stayed real close to me. Silas continued though, getting more persistent. I knew it was only a matter of time."

"So you fled."

She nodded again. "I'd seen the advertisement. It seemed the only answer."

He tightened his hold, bringing her back into the shelter of his arms. "You're safe now."

She touched his cheek, tipping his head down to meet her gaze. "I'm much more than that. I found love."

He met her kiss. When it broke, he cocked his head to the side. "So you never loved any of those men that asked for your hand?"

She smiled and shook her head. "No, none ever felt … right. They weren't you."

"Good to know." He brought her in for another kiss that grew ardent.

It was a while later before they walked together out to the barn with his arm around her. The new filly was still in the small paddock with her mother, all spindly legs with a fluffy copper coat.

"Oh, she's beautiful." Eliza gasped at the sight of her.

"Yeah, she turned out pretty nice, though her coat could change color. Her father was a dapple. She's got a lot of spirit though." He led her into the corral to make introductions.

"She'd better with a name like Liberty. That was nice of you letting Matthew name her."

"I hoped you'd appreciate it. I like Matthew, but honestly, I was hoping to snare the heart of his sister."

"You already had that, from the very first." She rose up and gave him a kiss. It was nice being able to do that and felt so natural and right. It was even better when his arms slid around her and he deepened the kiss.

It had to be a dream. Pleasure and love hummed

through her.

"Boss! There's smoke coming from the bull pasture!" The rushed call preceded the man that appeared around the corner of the barn.

Jerked apart and right into motion, Eliza ran with Cord around the side of the barn where they looked out to the southeast. Smoke rose up from the distant field. Two men swung onto horses and rode past them. Other men came out of the barn with shovels and hoes headed to their horses.

"Come on." Cord grabbed her hand dragging her into the barn. He grabbed her saddle, disappearing into a stall.

She realized he was saddling a horse for her. "Go, I can do that and follow."

"I'm not leaving you here alone and I'll need all the men there."

The stunning revelation froze her in her tracks until the need to help freed her. Still her mind couldn't get past the possibility. Surely he didn't think … Silas would set a fire to … he couldn't even know she was there. No one would tell him.

Cord had Lu saddled before the thought solidified in her mind with guilt and fear that she really had brought trouble to his ranch.

Eliza didn't worry about modesty getting her foot in the stirrup, but the skirt hampered her efforts to swing her leg over. She wished she'd been wearing her riding skirt but there was no way she was taking time to change. They had to get the fire out fast. Every second it grew, it damaged and endangered more of the ranch.

Proving Cord thought the same, he didn't bother with a saddle for himself. Just grabbing more digging implements, he swung on Rufus's bareback.

"Go on." She urged. "I'll be right behind you."

"Not without you." Cord stayed by her side.

Eliza pushed her horse faster than she'd ever ridden, prompted by the need to get there and the fact Cord wouldn't leave her.

"Be careful of the bulls," he called out to her. "They can be mean and unpredictable. The fire could have them stirred up."

"I'll be careful." She didn't want him distracted, worrying about her.

"Stay back from the flames with your skirt."

"Don't worry about me. I promise, I'll be careful."

Closer now, she could see the flames clearly. Instead of one big fire, there were four patches. The two smaller ones were between the creek and the grove of trees, just past the larger patches that were a good thirty to forty yards across and growing toward joining.

Cord pulled up, slid from his horse, and ran to join the men fighting the flames on the largest fire. The last two of his men came riding up. One joined in on the other larger fire while the other road past to attack one of the smaller, unmanned fires.

Eliza hung back feeling helpless as the men threw their efforts into fighting back the flames before the two fires joined and became so large they'd have no chance against it. With the men's attention focused on the large spots, she shifted hers to the smallest fire burning in the damp grass close by the creek.

A loud snort startled her as she slipped from her horse. She swung to face the huge bulls pushed back by the trees only about twenty feet away. Eliza stilled, never had she been so close to one of the large beasts. She'd seen them when they'd gone on the picnic to the lake but then, despite their size, they looked placid. Now tension poured from the beasts. She swallowed hard, tempted to call for Cord but the pressing need from the fire stayed her.

Glancing at the flames, she grabbed one of the heavy wool blankets that had been thrown over the back of her horse, and ran to the creek, casting it in the water while just hanging on to a corner as she'd seen the other man do. Out of the corner of her eye she saw a huge white and black beast shift her way, coming forward several feet. Nervous agitation evident in his movement and flaring nostrils.

"Easy," she muttered half under her breath. "I'm just trying to help."

The bull slammed one hoof into the ground then snorted and turned away.

Eliza blew out her breath and pulled the sodden blanket out. It had gained a considerable amount of weight and hefting it left her just as wet as it was, but she didn't let it slow her rushing to the flames. Heeding Cord's warning, she stopped short and tossed the sodden bundle. The fire made hardly a hiss as it was snuffed out. She pulled the blanket back and tossed it again over another area.

She repeated the process several more times, working around the edge of the fire, covering and snuffing out about a third of it before rushing back to the creek to rewet her blanket. By the time she made her third trip to the creek, she'd gone all the way around the edge of the fire and it was no longer growing.

Joseph, the hand who'd been working on the other small fire, came to join her.

"I can handle this one," she assured him.

He eyed it a moment, nodded and ran to help the men on the other blazes that had merged into one fire, but was losing ground as the men beat it down.

Eliza spared a glance to Cord. He feverishly drove his shovel into the ground and tossed dirt on the fire. Soot covered his face, but his movements didn't slow.

Turning back to what she was doing, she pulled her blanket back and threw it one more time over the last patch of burning grass, staunching the remaining flames. Wisps of smoke still rose from the blackened area. Eliza hurried back to the stream to wet the blanket once more to make certain there was no chance of any sparks kicking back up.

She froze at the loud snort to her right. Her heart

thundered. Fear warred with common sense to keep her from jerking around. Slowly she turned.

The bull had moved closer. It's head still high, but there was a glassy, angry look in its eyes.

"Easy." She repeated the word that had seemed to work earlier.

Its head swung side to side, almost in a negative motion.

"Cord," Eliza breathed out his name though she knew there was no way he could hear her. Fighting the impulse to run, she carefully slid one foot back then shifted to the next, easing away.

She jerked when the bull puffed out a breath, but continued her backward movement, putting more distance between them. She froze when the bull stiffened, its body so taunt it nearly broke through her common sense, and sent her fleeing before she realized the animal wasn't focused on her.

Alert, she heard sounds of grass rustling behind her and looked back.

She only caught a blur of a brown wool sleeve before a beefy hand clamped over her mouth muffling the scream that erupted from her as Silas Marsh wrapped his other arm around her body, trapping her arms to her side. The acrid smell of sweat and tobacco stung her senses over the smoky smell of the burning grass. Terror along with nausea roiled within.

"Defy me! Strike me!" He hissed in her ear as he pulled back toward the trees. It took a second for her mind to clear of shock and she began to fight.

No! He couldn't get her. Not now, not here. She was safe here.

Out of the corner of her eye she could see Cord and his men, but with their attention focused on the flames they might as well have been miles away. Swinging her head from side to side, she almost managed to rip free before his hand tightened, pulling her head back, cutting off her air to the point everything blurred around her.

Cord! She screamed but couldn't get anything out but the tears that leaked from her eyes. She tried to bite down on his hand, but couldn't budge her jaw. Dropping her legs from under her, she pitched forward, almost breaking his hold and pulling him to the ground. At the last second before they pitched over, his tree trunk thick legs found their footing. He lifted her off the ground, giving her a rough shake.

She whimpered into his hand. Still, she gained a little room to move. She threw her elbow back catching him in the stomach, rewarding her with a grunt that spurred her on. Her first two efforts in trying to kick him met with just air, but the third connected solidly with his shin. Eliza was unprepared when the hand on her mouth fell away and Silas spun her around. His hand swept out knocking away the scream before it could fully form past a squeak.

The blow knocked her to the ground. She was hauled right back up. Too shocked to do anything, Eliza watched the next blow coming.

Chapter Fifteen

Desperation poured from Cord as he drove the shovel into the hard packed ground and threw it onto the flames. Smoke made his eyes water and choked the air from his lungs. He tried not to think of the patches of burnt ground, but it was impossible. Luckily, none of his livestock were in any danger. He glanced over at his bulls and froze.

His yearling bull stood tense, focused at the edge of the trees. Its head up in obvious agitation. Worrisome, but not surprising, especially when the young bull was the most unpredictable of all his animals.

Concern had him shifting his gaze to Eliza. Where she'd been a moment earlier was empty. In an instant his eyes honed in on her even though her blue-green dress blended in with the trees closing around her.

The sight of the man dragging her toward the trees wiped all thought of the fire and his land from his mind. Anger as he'd never known exploded in him as one of Silas Marsh's large, beefy hands swung out and struck Eliza, knocking her to the ground.

"Eliza!" His burst into a run at the same time the young bull charged.

Fear for her spilt between the unstable bull and the just as unstable man. Making up his mind which was the greatest danger, Cord waved his arms and yelled. The bull stopped and turned his direction, but held its ground.

Marsh had a hand locked on Eliza's arm once more,

dragging her toward the trees. She dug her feet into the ground while she clawed at the fingers trapping her wrist, but her attempts to free herself had no effect on her stepfather's hold.

"Let her go." Cord yelled, discounting the bull and heading for what he figured was the true beast.

Silas's reacted by jerking Eliza back, ripping a pained cry from her.

Cord's heart jumped. He fought to wipe her fear and all thoughts of the bull from his mind. He covered the distance in a full out run.

Marsh released Eliza just before the impact, shoving her away. Cord plowed into the man who though shorter and slightly overweight, wasn't all fat. It was like connecting with a wall.

They stumbled back several feet, but didn't go down. Silas's beefy arms wrapped around Cord like steel bands, squeezing air from him. Cord grappled to shove him back, but only got enough distance between them to send a fist into the man.

Marsh groaned and shifted his hold. Releasing one hand, Silas brought it up to clamp around Cord's neck, squeezing down. "You've touched her, haven't you?" Marsh ground out.

"She's ... my wife."

"No." Fury burst in the man. Silas got his other hand up, locking on his neck. "No!"

Eliza cried out and threw herself on the man's back, jerking his attention away. Marsh turned on her, striking out. Cord managed to grab his arm stopping the blow, but Eliza was still knocked back to the ground.

"Temptress!" Silas Marsh yelled, any semblance of sanity frayed. "Harlot." He surged toward her.

Cord held him back.

"Wanton creature. Devil's mistress."

"Marsh!" Cord yelled, spinning the man away, placing

himself between Marsh and Eliza. "Get away from her."

The man looked up, tears in his eyes. "No! She's mine."

"Never," Cord vowed.

Rage distorted Marsh's features. "If not mine, then no man's." He yanked a derringer from his pocket.

Cord dodged to the side, expecting to hear the sharp crack of the gun and feel the bullet rip into him. But before Marsh could fire, the thunder of hooves pounding into the ground drew Marsh's attention. He turned a second before the bull hit him. The gun went off as Marsh flew back. The bull kept going over top of the man. It turned catching Marsh with its horns throwing him a good eight feet. Silas cried out then hit the ground with a sickening crash and fell silent.

The bull ambled forward, dipped his head shoving at the body one more time, then as if satisfied, it shifted toward Eliza. Cord stood, putting himself between her and the irate animal. For a minute it became a stare down, then with a final snort, it walked away.

Cord turned and reached Eliza pulling her up into his arms. She sank against him, wrapping her arms around his waist, burying her face into his neck. He held her, trying to calm his pounding heart.

She was all right. He said the words over and over again in his mind, but it didn't want to sink in. Finally, unable to help himself, he pushed her back enough to lower his head and cover her mouth with his. He drank her in, savoring the life and taste of her until he filled himself with the reality of her.

When he finally broke away, his heart pounded for a wholly different reason. She looked dazed, but when her fingers came up to caress his jaw and a smile bowed her sweet lips. He kissed the delicate appendages.

Brushing back her hair, he studied the reddening area on her chin where Marsh had struck her. She would have a bruise but nothing more. Still, it tore at him. Bringing his hand up, he fingered the area gently so not to cause her pain.

"I'm all right." The words trembled from her. Nothing was sweeter to him then when she turned her head slightly and kissed his finger just as he'd done hers an instant before and his world righted. He tipped his head down to rest his forehead against hers, just taking in the rightness of holding her safe in his arms.

"You're all right," he breathed the words out loud.

"Yes. Thanks again to you."

"Not me." It hit him, pulling his attention up. He glanced to where Silas Marsh lay broken on the ground.

Thomas Young stood over the large form. He looked up from him and shook his head. "He's dead," Thomas said, affirming the obvious.

Cord nodded. He heard Eliza's sharp intake of air and drew her to him so she didn't have to see the body.

She pulled away. "Cord!" Panic heightened her voice.

Cord spun, pushing her behind him but she stepped away as the bull staggered several steps toward them then dropped to its knees with a loud groan.

Cord released her and cautiously went to the animal. Blood coated the white tuft on its neck. As he approached, it made an effort to stand, only to collapse back on its side, chest heaving with labored depth.

Cord laid a hand on the large snout and stroked. The bull let out a final sigh and the massive chest fell still.

"No!" Eliza cried out, dropping to the ground beside the beast. Her hand trembled as she reached out caressing the bull's large head in much the same manner as she had him. Tears filled her. "No," she whispered. She turned to him, tears swimming in her beautiful blue eyes. "I'm so sorry."

He caught her fingers, bringing them to his heart. "It's all right."

"But, your bull." She cried out and looked around. The fire was out leaving only a small piece of smoldering, scorched land. She trembled. "The fire. It's all because of me." Anguish poured from her.

"No," he said firmly. Placing his hand under her chin, he forced her to meet his gaze. "No. But no matter what, I'd give it all up for you. Know that." He leaned forward catching her mouth again. Instead of taking her in, he gave of himself, of his life, of the truthfulness in his words.

"Let's get you home," he said, when he finally broke the kiss. Standing, he eased her up, his arm wrapping around her waist, pulling her tight to him.

Before he could stop her, she glanced toward Silas Marsh's body on the ground. "I'll have to send a message to my stepmother letting her know."

"I'll have one of the men ride into town. We'll have to let Cal know."

"I feel bad for her. She's a widow again. Though this time I don't think she'll be so upset. He wasn't a nice man, still …"

"I know, but as I said, it wasn't your fault."

Eliza nodded and fell silent a second. "You know, I can't say I'm sorry either. Otherwise, I never would have come here and I never would have met you. Nothing will ever make me regret that. When I saw the advertisement, I thought it was my chance for a new life, but I never guessed it was my chance for love."

Cord kissed her again, sealing her love with his as fate had deemed.

About the Author

I grew up in a small town in Wyoming loving the outdoors, sports, art, and reading Hardy Boys books. After reading them all at least a half dozen times, I started writing my own stories.

Thirty years ago I married a wonderful, honorable man. I'm mother of five children and grandmother of six boys. I love traveling. Through my husband's work and vacations, I have visited much of the United States, all over Eastern Europe, Canada, Mexico, China, Thailand, Cambodia and Australia, giving me many intriguing locations and experiences for my stories.

I am a storyteller. I write the classic hero story because I think there's a need for more heroes, love, and adventure in our lives. I'm not out to change the world with my writing; I'm just hoping to make your day a little better.

Hope you enjoy.
Alysia S. Knight

Please feel free to visit me through my website:

WWW.ALYSIASKNIGHT.COM